Dorran is done with investigating murders. He always ends up wounded, and it's not good for his health. But when Eli's brother approaches him and asks him to look into the stalker who's harassing his girlfriend, Dorran can't say no. He's still trying to get Eli's family to like him, and this is the perfect way, even though he's wary.

There are several suspects, but none of them fit the idea Dorran has of stalkers. Is he missing something? Is the stalker closer than he thought? Or has he gotten everything wrong? This time, there are no ghosts to interrogate, and Dorran is on his own.

False Friends
Copyright © 2020 Catherine Lievens
ISBN: 978-1-4874-2938-6
Cover art by Angela Waters

Published by eXtasy Books Inc or
Devine Destinies, an imprint of eXtasy Books Inc

Look for us online at:
www.eXtasybooks.com or www.devinedestinies.com

FALSE FRIENDS
LOST IN TRANSLATION BOOK 5

BY

CATHERINE LIEVENS

DEDICATION

False friends: in translation, letters or words that sound or look similar in two different languages but greatly differ in meaning.

CHAPTER ONE

The bathroom door slammed, jerking Dorran out of sleep. He opened his eyes, already scowling even though it was so early in the morning. He could tell by the light coming in through the window.

"Sorry," Eli said.

Dorran grumbled. "Not a problem."

"Try to get back to sleep."

Dorran softly snorted and buried his face against his pillow. That was easier said than done. Eli was used to getting up early to go to work. Hell, he was used to getting up in the middle of the night when he had a new case. Dorran, on the other hand, wasn't. That was one of the perks of working from home and making his own hours. He could get up when he wanted, which was what he did — or what he used to do anyway. Now, Eli had moved in with him, and they were still trying to find a way to mesh their lives.

There was a rustling on the sheets, and Dorran opened one eye to see Princess Butterfly looking at him. He grinned and hooked an arm around the cat, dragging her closer. She purred and settled against his chest, and together, they drifted back to sleep. Dorran knew he wouldn't be able to fall deeply asleep again, though. He never could, not once he had woken up, especially when he'd awakened because of a slamming door.

Dorran rubbed his fingertips over the cat's head. She was Eli's cat, but she loved Dorran just as much, which was a relief. Dorran had never had a pet, and he hadn't been sure what to do with her in the beginning. Now, she was already at home in his apartment, much more than Eli.

Dorran listened to Eli as he moved around in the bathroom. He smiled because even though he and Eli were still trying to find their way with each other and to settle in to living together without killing each other, he was happy. It was all he'd ever wanted since the two of them were teenagers. He'd broken up with Eli when they were kids, but he'd regretted it, even though he knew it was the right thing at the time. Things were different now, and he couldn't have been happier.

He and Eli had moved in together, and Eli's family was finally accepting Dorran. He hadn't thought it would happen, but even Eli's mother seemed to be happy with Dorran's presence in her son's life. He doubted she would throw them a wedding party or anything like that, but as it was, things were going well.

Dorran was surprised when the next time he opened his eyes, he could tell several hours had passed. He listened, but the apartment was quiet, a sure sign that Eli was at work. The cat wasn't there, either. She was probably in the kitchen or the living room, staring out the window at passersby on the street or sunning herself. Dorran had been abandoned, but he didn't blame her for it.

He stretched, pushing away the blankets. He had no idea what time it was, but from the sun streaming in through the window, it was about time to get up and start working.

He was looking forward to it. His life in the past several weeks had been a mess. There had been the move. But before that, there was the reunion with his father, finding out he had a kid sister, and his father being accused of murder. Angus had been innocent, but it had taken a while for things to settle down. Some days it felt like they still weren't, but Dorran could deal with it. He'd dealt with a lot worse.

He got to his feet, stretched again, and headed to the

bathroom, only to freeze when he stepped inside.

The room was a mess. Eli's pajama pants were on the floor, surrounded by wet towels. Water had sprayed out of the shower onto the floor, and Dorran almost slipped in it. The only reason he didn't fall on his face was that he managed to grab the doorframe. The toothpaste was open on the sink, a white blob on the ceramic. Eli's electric toothbrush was there, too, abandoned next to the faucet instead of on its base.

Dorran gritted his teeth. This was one of the things he wasn't yet used to. He wasn't a neat freak, but Eli was a slob, and there was no denying that. It was one of the reasons they were still trying to find their way around each other. Even though Dorran didn't demand that everything be perfect in the apartment, he also didn't want their home to look as if pigs lived with them. He understood Eli was in a rush when he left home in the morning, but that didn't mean he couldn't put the cap back on the toothpaste tube.

He huffed, then carefully stepped into the room, avoiding the puddles.

It took him about ten minutes to clean up. He hung the wet towels, put the pajama pants into the laundry basket, and dried the puddles. He also scrubbed the sink, since it was dirty with toothpaste. The entire time, he was scowling.

He relaxed once he was done and going through his morning routine. Eli was always in a rush in the morning, usually because he enjoyed staying in bed for far too long and snoozed his alarm at least twice. He cleaned when he came home, but Dorran worked in the apartment, and the bathroom couldn't be in this state. He couldn't jump around water puddles to get to the toilet for the entire day.

Once he was done, he grabbed his phone from the nightstand. He texted Eli, pointing out that he had cleaned the bathroom. Then he headed to the kitchen, smiling when he found there was a pot of coffee already made. It was still warm, and he took one of the mugs in the cupboard as his phone vibrated.

I'll clean up when I come home, Eli had written.

Dorran scowled at the words. *I know you will. But I still have to go to the bathroom for the entire day, and I'd rather not slip in one of the puddles and break my nose.*

The three dots wavered on the screen.

Sorry. I'll do better next time. Eli had added a winking emoji, and Dorran found himself smiling.

He'd been angry, and he still was, in a way. He realized that both he and Eli were having a hard time, though. They were used to living alone. Dorran had been on his own since he'd left his mother's apartment to go to college, and it wouldn't be easy for him to get used to having someone else around—someone who did things differently and who wasn't as neat as he was. He supposed he would get used to it, though. People usually did. There were millions of couples in the world, and most of them lived happily ever after once they moved in together. Surely he and Eli could have the same thing.

Dorran realized he would have to compromise, and he knew he could do it. He was happy with Eli, and he didn't want to lose that or to fight. Still, he couldn't be the only one who made an effort, and he would make sure that Eli knew that.

You think you're cute, he wrote.

I know I am. That's why you love me.

Dorran rolled his eyes. *I certainly don't love you because you leave a mess in the bathroom in the morning.*

I already told you I would clean up. I'm sorry, but I was in a rush.

I understand that. I might work from home, but it doesn't mean I don't understand the needs of a full-time job, especially a job such as yours. Dorran paused, trying to find his words. He didn't want to make Eli angry, not when his own anger was already fading. *But we live together now. We have to think of the other. Leaving everything as it is wasn't a problem when you lived on your own, but I have to use the bathroom for the entire day.*

You're right. Again, I apologize. I'll see you when I come home, okay? I have to go.

Dorran eyed the text. Was Eli angry? He couldn't tell from the words on the screen. *Stay safe*, he answered.

Always. Love you.

Dorran smiled. Eli wasn't angry. They would work this out like they always did. They might fight and grumble, but they loved each other, and that was what mattered.

Having Eli be home for dinner was still strange. He'd come to Dorran's apartment several times when they were dating, of course, and he'd stayed for the night. This was different, though, and it still made Dorran's stomach flutter in nervousness. Eli wasn't going anywhere. He was living with Dorran right now, and they were happy.

Or at least, they were happy until Eli saw what was on his plate and wrinkled his nose.

Dorran took a deep breath. He didn't want to fight, especially not after this morning. "Is something wrong?" he asked.

Eli pushed a broccoli head toward the edge of the plate with his fork. "You know I don't like broccoli."

"But I do."

"How can you? It tastes like feet."

Dorran arched a brow. "Do you have a foot fetish? How do you know what feet taste like?"

A light blush appeared on Eli's cheeks. "I don't have a foot fetish. And I don't know what feet taste like. Broccoli tastes like feet smell, though."

Dorran didn't push. It wouldn't end well if he did. "Don't eat it, then. You can still have the meat. Or don't you like that, either?"

"I like steak."

He'd come home early for once, and Dorran was happy. He focused on his own plate, not wanting the fight to continue. "Anything new at work?" he asked.

Eli shrugged one shoulder as he cut his meat. "Nothing much." He narrowed his eyes and looked at Dorran. "Nothing you need to stick your nose into."

Dorran would have been offended, but he couldn't be, not with all the murders he'd been involved in recently. "I'm not going to stick my nose into anything that isn't translating. I promise."

"And I believe you believe that, but for some reason, murder seems to find you, so I'm not sure I can believe you'll be okay."

"I haven't left the apartment today. Murder can't find me here, not when I'm hiding."

Eli chuckled and gave Dorran's hand a quick squeeze. "Do I have to remind you of the time your neighbor's boyfriend was killed?"

He didn't. "I had nothing to do with that." Not until Emanuel, Dorran's neighbor, had come knocking on his door and begged for help.

"How many other neighbors do you have?"

"Too many," Dorran grumbled, because Eli wasn't wrong. Murder and bad guys seemed to find him effortlessly, and he wished it would stop.

No matter what Eli and other people believed, Dorran didn't enjoy doing this. He didn't enjoy having people he cared for and loved accused of murder, especially when they hadn't actually done anything. He *really* didn't enjoy murderers coming after him because they were afraid he was going to find them and hand them over to the police.

No. The fact that he wasn't the best with people was one of the reasons he worked from home. That wouldn't change.

Eli got to his feet. "I'm grabbing some coffee. Do you want

some?" he asked.

Dorran shook his head. "You won't sleep tonight if you drink coffee now," he pointed out.

"So?"

Since Dorran wasn't Eli's mother, he didn't push. If Eli had trouble sleeping, it wasn't his problem. Eli was an adult, and he could take care of himself, just like he had when they hadn't been living together.

"Why is my mug dirty?" Eli asked from the kitchen.

"Oh, sorry. I used it this afternoon." Dorran should have rinsed it and put it in the dishwasher, but he'd forgotten it in the sink.

Eli appeared, mug in his hand. "Why did you use it? You know it's mine, and that it's my favorite."

Dorran frowned. "So? It's just a mug."

"It is, but it's mine. You shouldn't use it."

"And you shouldn't leave the bathroom the way you left it this morning, yet you did it," he snapped.

Eli glared at Dorran. "I've already apologized for that, and I told you I would clean tonight."

"You *did* say you would clean up tonight, but I pointed out that I have to use the bathroom during the day, and I don't want to go through an obstacle course every time I have to pee." Dorran snapped his mouth shut. What were they doing? They were fighting over wet towels and a mug. It was stupid. They needed to compromise, and since Eli probably wasn't going to take the first step, Dorran should.

He took a deep breath. "I apologize," he said.

Eli blinked at him. He'd probably been riling himself up for a good fight, but now it drained out of him. "You apologize for using the mug?"

Dorran nodded. "And for cooking broccoli. You're right. I know you don't like it, and I should avoid cooking it for dinner. If I want to eat it, I can eat it for lunch, when you're not home. I won't do it again."

Eli slowly stepped closer to the table and slid back into his chair. "This is weird," he said.

Dorran chuckled. "A bit, yes. But you're not going anywhere, and neither am I. You still want to live with me, don't you?"

Eli put the mug on the table and took one of Dorran's hands. "Of course I want to live with you."

"Then we'll have to compromise. We have to realize that some things are important for the other, and we have to deal with that. We're going to drive each other crazy if we don't, and we'll be unhappy. That's the last thing I want. So again, I apologize for using your favorite mug, and I won't use it again."

"And I promise I'll try to keep the bathroom clean in the morning."

"That's all I ever wanted," Dorran said with a grin. It was a start, at the very least. He had no doubt they would find more things that bothered them eventually, but if they could talk about it the way they just had, they would be okay.

Eli grinned. "*All* you ever wanted?" he asked, the lilt of his voice making what he was talking about obvious.

Dorran leaned closer to Eli, wondering if they could make it to the couch or if they might just have sex on the dining table when a face appeared behind Eli. "Are you done yelling?" Francis asked. "Oh. It looks like you're getting on with the program. Will you be having sex on the dining table or on the couch?"

That was too close to what Dorran had been thinking. He grabbed his fork and threw it at Francis' head, but of course, since Francis was a ghost, it passed right through it. Francis scowled at him and raised his hands. "I was just asking."

"Leave us alone," Dorran said. Then, he turned his attention back to Eli.

The next time he looked up, Francis was gone, which was a good thing, since Dorran was already missing his shirt and being kissed senseless. He could focus entirely on Eli now, and he did just that.

CHAPTER TWO

This time, Dorran didn't wake up because of the bathroom door slamming. He wasn't sure *what* had woken him, but he rolled to his back and stretched, smiling when he heard Eli was still in the bathroom. Dorran seldomly managed to open his eyes this early, but things had been slowly changing since Eli had started spending the nights with him. Now, he was beginning to see it wasn't a bad thing. He might be early, but if he started working in the next hour or so, it also meant that he would be done with his daily work early. It wasn't a bad thing at all.

Eli stepped out of the bathroom and blinked at seeing Dorran awake. "I'm sorry. Did I wake you up?" he asked.

Dorran eyed Eli's naked chest, wondering if they had time for a quickie. Probably not. "Nope. I guess I'm not tired anymore."

Eli laughed. "You, not tired? I didn't think such a thing was possible."

Dorran grabbed Eli's pillow from next to him, then threw it at his boyfriend.

Eli laughed as he caught it and dropped it back onto the bed before reaching for his shirt. "By the way, my mom called."

Dorran had to resist the urge to groan. "Yeah? How is she?"

"Good. She wanted to know if we're coming to Sunday lunch."

It was a tradition for Eli's family. Dorran didn't understand it, but he realized that was because his family was very different from Eli's. He had regular contact with his sister, and now, with his brother and his father. But his mother was an alcoholic, and the only time Dorran saw her was when he cleaned her apartment. There hadn't been Sunday lunches in his family.

Eli's family was another story, though. They had Italian origins, and Eli's mother was proud of them. It wasn't a huge family — there were three children, Eli and his two brothers — but their mother always cooked for an army, and even though she was still uncomfortable around Dorran, she was more than happy to feed him. Dorran wasn't exactly looking forward to going to lunch, though. The rest of Eli's family was fine, but Eli's mother always looked at him as if she expected him and Eli to start having sex on the dining table.

Which they *had* done last night, so maybe she wasn't wrong.

But Dorran knew things wouldn't get better if they didn't get to know each other, so he nodded. "We're going," Dorran confirmed. Even if the company wasn't the greatest, it was good food, and it was one more day that Dorran didn't have to cook. He would always say yes to someone else cooking for him since he hated spending time in the kitchen.

Eli's pleased smile told Dorran he'd said the right thing. "I'll text her and tell her we'll be there."

"Ask her if we need to bring anything."

Eli rolled his eyes. "We don't. You know that. She'll get offended if you try."

"It's the polite thing to do."

Eli sat on the edge of the mattress and rubbed Dorran's knee through the blanket. "It's polite if you visit someone you don't usually see, but this is family. You don't have to be polite. You just have to be yourself."

That was easier said than done. Dorran doubted he and

Eli's mother would ever be best friends, but then they didn't need to. They were both in Eli's life to stay, which meant that they had to tolerate each other, something they had finally managed to do. Dorran knew she was uncomfortable with the fact that Eli was with a man, but she seemed to have accepted it, and she hadn't talked about him having kids in a while. Dorran was relieved. He and Eli weren't anywhere close to being ready to talk about that, let alone do it.

Eli leaned closer and kissed Dorran. "I wish I could get back into bed with you," he murmured.

Dorran wriggled his eyebrows. "You could."

Eli sighed. "I can't. Mel already called me, and he's waiting for me."

Dorran sighed and dropped back onto his pillow. "Work always wins," he said dramatically.

The corners of Eli's eyes crinkled. "You knew how much I work before you agreed to move in with me," he pointed out.

Dorran threw his arm over his eyes. "You're married to your job. I'll always be the mistress."

Eli chuckled and used the pillow Dorran had thrown at him earlier to thump Dorran on the head. "You're a goof."

Dorran peeked at him. "*Your* goof."

Eli's smile widened. "That's right. You're all mine." He checked his watch. "But all of this is going to have to wait, because I have to go." He leaned over and kissed Dorran again, then got to his feet.

Dorran listened to him move around the apartment, a smile on his face. Things might not always be easy for them, but they were getting easier, and more importantly, they were working.

He grabbed his phone. Maybe he could catch up with his best friend while Charlie was commuting between home and work. Charlie hated public transport, so he wouldn't mind texting.

What are you up to? he sent. Then he rose from the bed and headed to the bathroom. He blinked when he saw that the towels were hung and the floor was dry. Well, dry-ish. His phone vibrated in his hand, and he checked the text.

What everyone else in the city is doing. Going to work. You?

Dorran took a selfie of himself, still in his pajamas. *Same.*

I hate you.

Dorran sent a winking emoji. *You love me.*

You're right. I do.

"What are you smiling about in the bathroom? The size of your dick? Because I have to say, it's not as disappointing as I first thought it would be," Francis said.

Dorran jerked, almost dropping his phone in the toilet, which Eli had left open. He twirled around, glaring at the ghost. "You know you shouldn't do that," he said.

Francis leaned his shoulder against the doorframe. "Do what?"

"Appear like you just did and scare me to death. I hate it."

"I need to keep you on your toes."

"You need to be careful before I decide to exorcise you. Now shoo. I need to use the bathroom."

"Why did you take your phone with you? You have to use the bathroom, yet that thing is always in your hand."

Dorran rolled his eyes. "You're showing your age, Francis. Can you please get out? I really need to go. And no peeking!"

Luckily, Francis obeyed. His reactions to Dorran and Eli were always unpredictable, especially now that he was almost another human being. Well, he'd always been a human being, but since a considerable of time had passed since Francis had died, Francis was becoming more and more visible every day. Dorran still couldn't touch him, and he knew he'd never be able to. Francis was dead, no matter how real he looked. But having him in the apartment was like having a roommate, and Dorran didn't mind, especially since Francis could disappear when Dorran needed him to.

His life was strange. There was no denying that. He wouldn't change it for anything in the world, though. He had his boyfriend, a cat, and a ghost roommate. He doubted anyone else could say the same.

Dorran wasn't surprised to see Eli come home dragging Mel with him. Eli had texted him to let him know, and Dorran had made sure to cook enough for three.

Mel was Eli's partner. They were a great team, and Dorran liked Mel. The problem was that Mel was awkward around him ever since he'd discovered he could see ghosts. Dorran had nothing to do with the gift, and he wished Mel could understand that.

Still, since Mel's wife was out of town, Dorran wasn't about to let him die from hunger, or worse, eat take out for the entire time. He smiled at Mel, hoping that Mel would see that he was happy to see him. "You should have come sooner," he said.

Mel looked away and shrugged. "Don't see why. I can feed myself."

Dorran grimaced. "That's not what I was saying. I know you can feed yourself. I wasn't trying to be rude."

"You weren't," Eli said. He kissed Dorran's cheek, then turned to glare at Mel. "He's just grumpy. He always is when his wife is out of town."

But they both knew there was more to it than that.

Mel and Dorran had never been friends, but since Eli and Dorran had started dating, Mel had become part of Dorran's life. They saw each other fairly often, and they were usually pretty relaxed. But Mel had been there when Carole and Dorran had spoken to the last murder victim Dorran had dealt with. Dorran's father had been suspected of killing his mother-in-law, and Dorran had talked to her to find out if it was the truth. It hadn't been, but unfortunately, Mel had been there, and he'd seen what was happening. He'd realized he could see ghosts, and he was probably still freaking out about it. Dorran understood that. He'd freaked out himself when he'd found out, too. But eventually he'd stopped, and he'd worked on his power to be able to control it. Mel would have to do the same eventually. Otherwise, the ghosts were going to start bugging him in his everyday life, and he would have a hard time working.

Of course, Mel didn't know that, because he refused to talk to Dorran about it.

Dorran knew why. Mel associated him with being able to see ghosts, and it made sense, since he'd been there. He hadn't seen Mel since then, and he was surprised Eli had forced him to come for dinner. He might not be aware of just how uncomfortable Mel was, but he wasn't blind, and he was a detective, after all. He knew something was up between Dorran and Mel, yet he was blissfully ignoring it.

"Eli called me, so I made sure to cook things you like," Dorran told Mel.

Mel rubbed the back of his neck. "You shouldn't have. Actually, I should probably go home."

"You're not going anywhere," Eli said. "Dorran cooked, and you're not going to offend him by running away. Come on. I don't know about you, but I'm starving."

They settled around the table, each of them with their own plate. Dorran had made sure not to cook broccoli this time, and he listened as Eli and Mel talked about their case. In the beginning they wouldn't have, but after everything Dorran had been through, they didn't try to keep things hidden from him anymore. Besides, he'd promised he wouldn't get involved. He was done with murders and murderers. They were dangerous for his health.

It was awkward. Eli tried to fill the silence, but it wasn't easy, not when Mel only answered with grunts every time the conversation turned to something that wasn't their job.

Dorran was relieved when he could rise from the table and head to the kitchen to clean up, but of course, Eli thwarted his plan. He followed him there, then gave him a hip-bump. "Go talk to him," he murmured.

Dorran shook his head. "He doesn't want to talk to me. I'm not a detective, but even I can see that."

"Of course he doesn't want to talk to you. You were there when he discovered he could see ghosts. I can only imagine how that would feel. But you do need to talk. He needs to realize that he can't ignore this forever."

Dorran blinked. "You know about that?"

"I would be offended if I hadn't been acting as if you seeing ghosts wasn't a tragedy in the beginning. But yes, I know that eventually, the ghosts will become too strong, and Mel won't be able to avoid this. I listen to you when you speak, Dorran. That's why I want you to talk to him. Besides, I don't like my boyfriend and one of my best friends being at odds."

Dorran couldn't get out of it. He would have preferred to allow Mel to come to him at his own pace, but Eli wasn't wrong. It wasn't just a ghost problem. Mel and Dorran were in each other's lives, and that wasn't going to change anytime soon. They should talk this out.

Dorran didn't want things to be awkward between the two of them. That was the main reason he left Eli in the kitchen to clean up and went to sit in the living room. Mel was on the edge of the couch, looking around as if he expected a ghost to pop out any second, and ready to jump to the door when it happened. And he wasn't wrong. With Francis around, it was a definite possibility.

Dorran cleared his throat. "So, Eli said your wife is out of town?"

Mel shrugged. "She's visiting family. Her parents."

"I see. And of course, you didn't go, because you had to

work."

"And because I'm not crazy about them. Work is more of an excuse than anything."

"I see."

Mel rubbed the back of his neck, then got to his feet. "I should go. You already did so much, cooking for me. I don't want to bother you any longer."

Dorran reached for him, but he didn't touch him. "You don't have to leave." He sucked in a breath. He didn't expect to solve their problem right now, but he needed to say something. "You can talk to me if you want. About the ghosts, I mean. I know you're uncomfortable, but I promise I had nothing to do with it. I mean, I didn't force you to see ghosts, or put a spell on you, or anything like that."

Mel dropped onto the couch and rubbed his face. "I know you didn't have anything to do with it."

"Yet you've been avoiding me."

"Because I can't do this. I'm a detective. No one would take me seriously if I started talking to ghosts."

Dorran bit his lower lip. "I'm not a detective, so I don't know how things will work when it comes to your job, but I can tell you that I've been through what you've been going through. I freaked out when I first found out what I could do." It had been when he and Eli had first reconnected, and when he'd first met Mel. "But ignoring it will only make things harder. That, I can promise you. I wish I could have ignored it, but now I know why I shouldn't have, and I'm glad I didn't. You don't have to learn to use your gift, although I can imagine it might be a tool for your job. But at the very least, you need to be able to shield yourself from the ghosts. They're going to drive you crazy if you don't."

Mel shook his head. "I'm not ready."

"And that's okay. Just keep in mind that you can talk to me anytime you want. I'll always be here, and I understand what you're going through. I can help you."

Mel looked at Dorran. "I don't know if anyone can help me. I can see ghosts, Dorran. That's not normal."

Dorran had to agree with him, although he wasn't sure it was a bad thing. It wasn't normal, sure, but then, normal was overrated.

CHAPTER THREE

Dorran was always nervous when he went to Sunday lunch with Eli's family. This time wasn't any different, even though things had been getting better. He knew what to expect, so he smiled when he stepped into the house, waving at Eli's father, who, like always, was sitting in his armchair watching football or whatever other sport he enjoyed. Dorran wasn't a sports guy, and even though he didn't hate watching sports on TV, he also wasn't that interested in it.

"Hey, Dad," Eli said as he dragged Dorran toward the living room.

Dorran wasn't surprised to see that Eli's brothers, Austin and Julian, were there. He smiled at them, shook their hands, and accepted a kiss on the cheek from Andrea, Julian's wife. There was also another woman there, someone he'd never met, and from the look of it, Eli hadn't, either.

"This is my girlfriend, Lacey," Austin said.

Dorran grinned at her. "I'm not the newest member of the family anymore, then," he said as he shook her hand.

She smiled at him, and he hoped they would get along. He didn't have it in him to fight with someone else, especially not when it came to Eli's family. "It's a pleasure to meet you," she said.

They settled into the living room while waiting for lunch to be ready. Dorran had tried helping Eli's mother several times in the past, but she always kicked him out of the kitchen, and he'd stopped. Eli had told him that she didn't like anyone invading her kitchen, not because it was her job to cook for the family, but because she wanted things done the way she did them, and no other way. No one was allowed in the kitchen when she cooked, not even Eli and his brothers, so Dorran had relented. It still made him feel guilty and like she was serving them, but even though he didn't understand her, he respected her and her decisions.

"So, Dorran," Lacey started. "Austin told me that Eli is a police detective?"

Dorran wasn't sure why she was asking him that, although he already knew Eli wouldn't talk to her about his job, so maybe Austin had warned her about that. "He is."

"And you're a translator?"

That, Dorran could talk about. "I am."

Lacey sighed. "It has to be so nice to speak more than one language. I took Spanish in school, but I can't remember anything."

Dorran was used to this kind of conversation. Most people said the same things to him when they realized he spoke more than one language. "Well, it's not easy," he said.

She was already moving on to something else, though. "Austin also told me that you were involved in several murder cases."

Dorran groaned. It was the last thing he wanted to talk about. "I was, but by accident. I didn't get involved because I wanted to."

"Of course not. Who wants to get involved in a murder case?" She shivered, and Dorran didn't point out that it was Eli's job to do that. "I was just wondering how you managed to solve those murders."

"By chance. I didn't set out to do it." But he'd had to.

"Really? How many have you solved by now?"

Dorran wished he could say he didn't keep track, but he remembered every single time his life had been in danger. "Four."

Lacey slowly nodded. "See? You're pretty good at that."

"It was all luck. I wouldn't have gotten involved if my brother and my father hadn't been accused of murder in two of those cases."

"So you only want to get involved when someone you know is suspected of being a murderer?"

"That's not what I was saying. But I'm not going to be involved anymore, because I'm staying far away from any kind of crime."

She laughed. "I bet you are. I would, too. It has to be terrifying to be involved in that kind of situation."

It was. Dorran felt much better having decided to stay away, and he knew Eli did, too. Of course, he'd never planned to get involved in the four murders he'd eventually solved, yet they'd found him. He hoped murder was done with him, but how could he know for sure?

Eli's mother came in, rescuing Dorran from the conversation. She grinned when she saw them together in the living room, then gestured toward the dining room. "Lunch is ready," she said. "Austin, you need to grab the drinks from the kitchen."

Austin jumped to his feet. Everyone obeyed her, and Dorran wasn't any different. He followed her orders to grab the napkins, then placed them on the dining table. The food was already there, weighing it down, and they settled around it, ready to eat.

Lunch was perfect, just like always, and Dorran ate way too much. Eli's mother always made an effort to include him in the conversation, but this time, she was also including Lacey, and it was different. It was as if Dorran was already part of the family, and he knew several of the stories she talked about because he'd already heard them. He belonged, even though he never expected that to happen. He wasn't sure how to feel about it, either. He was happy, but it felt strange.

He suspected that the strangest thing for him was to see a family happy together. He'd never had that, and he wasn't quite sure how to behave. Still, he wouldn't change it for anything in the world, so he focused on the food and the company instead of the past.

He felt better once lunch was over, even though he could barely walk. He didn't feel as much of a stranger anymore, and it helped that Eli was making an effort to remind everyone that they were a couple and not just two friends. He kept touching Dorran as they ate, and once they were done and leaned back into their chairs, he hooked an arm around Dorran's shoulders and pulled him close, kissing his temple. Dorran's cheeks felt hot, but he couldn't stop a stupid grin from appearing on his face.

"Why don't you go to the living room?" Austin told his parents. "We'll take care of the clean-up."

His mother opened her mouth, no doubt to protest, but Austin shook his head, and she huffed. "Fine. We'll go sit down. But call me if you need help," she ordered.

"I know how to clean up, Mom. I've been doing it for years," Austin pointed out.

Yet, as soon as their parents were gone, instead of cleaning up, he turned to Dorran and Eli. He opened his mouth, but Lacey grabbed his wrist and pulled him toward the kitchen.

Dorran frowned and looked at Eli. "What was that about?"

Eli shrugged. "I don't know, and I don't care. I don't want to think right now. I don't think I can, not when I feel so full."

Dorran chuckled and started to get up to help with the cleaning up, but Austin and Lacey reappeared. They looked nervous, and he knew they wanted to talk to him and Eli, something he wasn't looking forward to considering the conversation he and Lacey had had earlier.

"We'd like to meet you for dinner," Austin said.

Dorran blinked. That wasn't what he had expected. "Not tonight, I hope," he said.

Austin chuckled. "I don't think I'll be eating anything until tomorrow, so no. But maybe sometime during the week? Friday?"

Dorran and Eli looked at each other, and Dorran nodded. "Why don't you come to our place on Friday night?" Eli said. "We'll have dinner."

Austin nodded and looked relieved. Something was happening there, and Dorran already knew he wasn't going to like it.

"What do you think they want?" Dorran asked once he and Eli were in the car headed home.

Eli gave him a sideways glance. "Why do you think they want something?"

Dorran snorted. "Please. You can't tell me you haven't noticed how they whispered to each other, and Lacey asked me about your job and the fact that I've been involved in several murder cases."

Eli grimaced. "All right. Yeah, it's kind of obvious they want something. I have no idea what, though. You want me to text Austin and ask him before they come for dinner?"

Dorran was dying of curiosity, and he hated having to wait five entire days to find out what was happening. But since Austin and Lacey hadn't wanted to talk in front of the rest of the family and had insisted on a private meeting, he doubted they would explain over the phone. It had to be too important, and they'd decided on Friday. "No. But we're not going to like it, either of us," he said.

"I agree. Austin is family, though."

"If he has a problem with the law or something like that, he's probably going to need you, not me." And Dorran hoped that was the case. It might be selfish, but he'd come too close to dying too many times. He wasn't planning on doing that ever again. Of course, he wasn't sure he'd have a choice. Death seemed to find him, and so did murderers.

"I'm sure everything will be okay," Eli said.

Dorran wasn't sure he could go along with it, though. Things were never okay when murderers were involved, although hopefully, that wasn't the case here. Maybe Austin and Lacey just wanted to spend an evening with Dorran and Eli.

Dorran didn't believe that for one second.

Dorran was relieved when they arrived home. Sunday lunch was always a huge thing in Eli's family, which meant that while they did eat lunch there, they also stayed for most of the afternoon and part of the evening. It wasn't late, but Dorran couldn't wait to stretch out on the bed. He still felt too full from lunch, and he knew that sensation wouldn't fade anytime soon.

He toed his shoes off as soon as he got into the apartment, then picked them up and put them away. He arched a brow at Eli because he knew that Eli tended to leave his shoes right where he took them off, and Dorran had already tripped on them a few times on his way to the front door. Eli gave him a huge grin, then made a scene of picking them up and putting them away, too. Dorran chuckled and shook his head, then leaned over and kissed his boyfriend on the cheek. "You're lucky you're cute," he told him.

Eli wrapped his arms around Dorran. "I'm more than cute."

"Yeah, you are. You're also annoying, messy, sloppy —"

Eli shut Dorran up by kissing him. Dorran smiled into the kiss, leaning closer, wrapping his own arms around his boyfriend.

It was what he'd always wanted and what he'd missed for all those years. Now he had Eli back in his life, and he wasn't letting go. He didn't care if they fought about misplaced shoes and wet towels. He was in this forever.

"Why don't we head to the bedroom," Eli murmured.

"Tired already?" Dorran teased him.

"Yes. *So* tired. I can't wait to get in bed."

"Really? I thought you might want to watch a movie first."

Eli huffed, then dragged Dorran to the bedroom. "You're not as funny as you seem to think, Dorran."

"I'm hilarious."

"Keep thinking that."

Dorran loved this. He loved that he and Eli knew each other well enough to be able to tease the other without hurting him. He loved that they shared a bed every night, that they woke up together. Well, that only happened some days. Most days, only Eli woke up, and Dorran was left to an empty bed. Dorran's hours were changing even without him meaning to do it, though, and he knew it was because of Eli.

That was fine. It was one of the compromises they needed to make, and Dorran was more than happy to make it.

They fell onto the bed, wrapped around each other. Now that they lived together and had all the time in the world, they usually took things slow. Dorran didn't mind. He liked frantic, but he also loved kissing and feeling Eli's hands roaming over his body. He didn't mind taking his time, especially now that they had it.

Eli was gentle as he removed Dorran's clothes. If there was one thing Dorran could say about his boyfriend, it was that he always made him feel cherished and safe. No matter how many times Eli yelled at him, Dorran knew he would never hurt him.

He needed that. He hadn't realized it until recently, but even though his mother had never been violent with him, she'd still scared him. She used to scream at him, to insult him, and while he knew it was the alcohol talking, it didn't make it easier. He loved his sister and his brother, but they'd never given him what he needed. Eli did, though.

Eli was safe, and even when he was angry, he never insulted Dorran. He never raised a hand to him, and he never would. In his arms, Dorran was home, and he was never planning on leaving.

He didn't protest when Eli slithered down his body. He felt warm lips close around the head of his cock, and he closed his eyes, burying his fingers into Eli's hair.

He never protested when Eli took care of him, which was most of the time, at least in the bedroom. Dorran was a strong man in his everyday life, or at least he liked to think so. Here in the bedroom, though—in the most private room of their apartment—he could break down and allow Eli to take care of him. He didn't need to think, to be strong. He didn't need to keep up the mask he always wore, especially with other people. He didn't have to fake being happy or okay.

But he *was* okay right now, more than ever.

Dorran reached for Eli, wanting him close when they came. Eli resisted for a few seconds, but Dorran kept on pulling, and he finally gave in. He moved back up Dorran's body, kissing what felt like every inch of Dorran's skin as he did so. When he was up to Dorran's face, their lips brushing against each other, Dorran shuddered in pleasure.

He reached down, pulling their cocks together, wrapping his hand around them. It was a little dry, a little painful, but also perfect.

Eli helped him, pressing against him, wrapping one of his hands around Dorran's. They worked together to pleasure each other and themselves, and when they came, it was only seconds away from each other.

They flopped onto the mattress, and Dorran couldn't help the goofy smile on his lips. "That was nice," he said.

Eli scoffed. "Only nice? I'll have to work harder next time."

Dorran shook his head and rolled so he could press his

cheek against Eli's chest. "It was perfect." He kissed the skin next to Eli's nipple. "I love you."

Eli relaxed under Dorran's touch. "I love you too."

"And I love both of you and what I just saw," Francis said from somewhere in the bedroom.

Dorran groaned as Eli frantically tried to cover them both. "Francis, you know the rules," he said.

Francis didn't appear.

Dorran knew Francis had already figured out Eli would throw something at his head if he did.

"Fine," Francis said with a grumble. "I promise I wasn't here while you two were having sex. I'm just teasing you. Is that against the rules, too?"

Dorran shook his head, but he was smiling. "Go do whatever you do while we're sleeping. We'll talk tomorrow." It couldn't be easy to be a ghost and to have only a handful of people able to see you. Things were different now that Francis was stronger, but he still preferred to appear only to Dorran and Eli and a few others. It was probably a good thing, because most people would freak out, but it also meant that Francis was lonely.

"See you tomorrow," Francis said.

Then he was gone, and Dorran focused on his boyfriend.

CHAPTER FOUR

Dorran flitted around the kitchen, getting everything ready. He wasn't sure why it was important to him to make a good impression on Austin and Lacey, but it was.

"You know no one will care if the napkins aren't perfectly folded, right?" Eli asked from the living room.

Dorran leaned to the side so he could see Eli and glared at him. "I know. I want them to be perfect for myself, not for them."

Eli, who was sitting on the couch with his feet kicked up on the coffee table, rolled his eyes. "That's bullshit, and you know it. You're not nearly as neat when it's only the two of us."

"That's because it's only the two of us. This is different. And you could give me a hand."

Eli huffed, but he got up from the couch. Instead of helping Dorran, though, he wrapped his arms around Dorran from behind and leaned closer, kissing the back of Dorran's neck. "Things are already perfect," he murmured. "*You* are perfect. I don't need you to impress my brother. Whatever he thinks about you, and whatever he and his girlfriend need from us tonight, it's not going to change the way I feel about you. I love you, and I'm not going anywhere."

Dorran had to stop moving. He didn't turn around, not ready to look Eli in the eyes. "So you truly don't care if your family hates me? You wouldn't choose them over me?"

Eli took a second to answer, and Dorran held his breath, at least until he heard Eli's words. "They don't hate you," he

28

said.

"I know they don't. Even your mother seems to have accepted me. It was just hypothetical."

"Then you should stop thinking about that. But yes, I would still choose you. I know I didn't always, and I'm sorry we lost a lot of time because of that."

That had always been a point of contention between them when they were together the first time. It was why Dorran had broken up with Eli in the first place. He hadn't wanted to stay in the closet, and he'd thought that was where Eli was going to spend most of his life. He'd been adamant by then that he wasn't going to come out to his family or to anyone else, and Dorran had understood, but it hadn't been enough. He hadn't wanted to be a secret, and he'd left.

Now that he and Eli had found each other again, he wasn't a secret, and he was happy.

"I don't think we would have been the same if we hadn't broken up back then," he said.

"Maybe not. Maybe it was the best thing for both of us. I don't know, and I don't think it matters at this point. What does matter is that you don't have to impress my family or anyone else. I already love you. That's not going to change."

Dorran believed him. It was tempting to listen to the little voice in the back of his head telling him that Eli was just trying to keep him happy, that he didn't deserve to be loved, that if even his mother hadn't managed to do it, how could Eli? But Dorran knew better than to listen to it. He'd been fighting with it for most of his life, and now that he had Eli by his side, he knew he was stronger, so he turned around in Eli's arms and kissed him softly. "Why don't you help me get everything on the table. They're probably about to arrive."

Eli rolled his eyes, but he obeyed, and Dorran was grateful they weren't about to fight over how much food he'd cooked or how he'd set the table. He knew he'd gone over the top. He wanted to make a good impression, even though he didn't have to. Eli might not be planning to dump his ass if his family disliked him, but that didn't mean Dorran didn't *want* them to like him. They were going to be in each other's lives for a while—forever, if he had a say in it. He wanted to get along with Eli's family because he didn't want Eli to have to choose. He shouldn't have to, and Dorran was going to do everything he could to make sure he didn't.

There was a knock on the door, and he turned wide eyes to Eli. Eli shook his head, obviously amused, and went to open. While he was at the door, Dorran looked around, making sure Francis was nowhere to be seen. "I need you to stay away, please," he murmured. He'd wanted to tell the ghost sooner, but Francis hadn't been around today. "We can talk about everything that happens later, and you can listen in to the conversations. Just, please, don't show yourself."

Francis didn't answer, and Dorran hoped he'd heard him.

He plastered a smile on his face and went to greet Austin and Lacey.

Dinner was pretty much what every dinner between friends and family was. They sat at the table and ate. Dorran was pleased to see that Austin and Lacey seemed to appreciate what he'd cooked. They talked about nothing important—Austin and Eli's family, their jobs, how the apartment looked, how Eli and Dorran were dealing with each other now that they'd moved in together, and of course, Eli's cat, who made an appearance to beg for a piece of meat.

Dorran relaxed, and he thought that everything was going to be okay up until he grabbed the coffee from the kitchen. When he came back, he could see that Austin and Lacey had finally decided to explain why they were there. He sighed and sat back down at the table. He wasn't going to like it. He would need to go through it, though.

"So," Austin started. "The reason we wanted to have

dinner with you is that we need to talk to you."

Eli straightened in his chair. "What's going on? Are you okay?"

Austin nodded. "I'm fine. It has nothing to do with me, actually. It's Lacey." He looked at Lacey.

She swallowed, apparently not eager to talk. She did, though. "I think I have a stalker, and I don't know what to do."

Dorran hadn't expected that. To be honest, he wasn't sure what he'd expected from the conversation. It wasn't a stalker, though.

Eli turned his attention to her. "Can you give me more details?"

"It was small things in the beginning, like the feeling of being followed around. Someone called at work several times, asked for me, and hung up when I answered."

"Anything else?" Eli asked after Lacey didn't continue.

She looked at Austin. "Yes. I'm pretty sure stuff has been disappearing from my apartment."

Dorran felt his eyes widen. That didn't sound like a stalker. Well, the following around and maybe even the phone calls did, but having someone inside her apartment? It was terrifying, and Dorran could only imagine what she felt.

"Are you sure things are disappearing?" Eli asked.

"Not a hundred percent. It's like when you put something down and you can't find it later, you know? You're sure you put it there, but then, you find it in another place. Except I haven't found any of the things I've lost yet."

"So you're sure this is a stalker? I'm not trying to say that you're imagining things, but it can be easy to fool yourself into thinking someone is following you, especially if you're anxious."

"I've had all four my tires flat on my car at the same time," Lacey said. "The guy I called to pick up the car said that someone slashed them. All four of them. That's not my imagination."

Eli frowned. "You're right. It's not. What do you need from us, though? I work homicide, not this kind of case. I don't think I can help you."

"What do you mean you can't help her?" Austin snapped. "What are you going to do, wait for her to get hurt or killed?"

Lacey cleared her throat, getting Austin's and Eli's attention before they could start fighting. "I realize that you probably wouldn't be able to do anything," she told Eli. "But what about Dorran?"

Dorran blinked. His first instinct was to say *hell, no,* but he didn't want to rush into this and hurt Lacey. "I'm not a policeman," he says.

"This doesn't sound like such a bad idea, actually," Eli said. Dorran blinked at him. Had he heard those words come out of his boyfriend's mouth? Eli gave him a sheepish smile, then explained, "I can't do anything, and I agree with Austin that if Lacey goes to the police, they're going to tell her they can't help because nothing has happened to her yet. It's unfortunate, but it's the state of things. You have a good instinct, though, and I can help, even though not officially."

Dorran wanted to say no. This was what he'd been trying to stay out of, but how could he? Lacey was his brother-in-law's girlfriend. Dorran didn't want to start a relationship with her by not helping her, especially when she might be in danger.

He sighed. "Fine. I'm not making any promises, because this isn't my job, but I'll look into it." And he was sure he would regret it, too.

CHAPTER FIVE

Lacey and Dorran were meeting for lunch, and Dorran wasn't looking forward to it. He'd agreed to help Lacey, and he'd been second guessing it ever since. He wanted to find a way to get out of it, but he doubted he would.

He and Eli had talked about it, and Eli had confirmed there was little the police could do. Lacey didn't seem to have any idea who her stalker was, and they couldn't just arrest people at random, just like they couldn't put her under protection. So far, she hadn't been hurt, and unfortunately, they would wait until she was to step in—if they did at all. Dorran despised it, but as Eli had said, it was the state of things, and there was nothing he could do about it.

So here he was, meeting Lacey for lunch in a café. Dorran wasn't looking forward to eating anything. The thought of getting involved in one more of these cases made his stomach churn, but at the very least, he needed to listen to Lacey. She hadn't gone into many details when they'd talked at dinner the week before, and they hadn't mentioned anything during Sunday lunch, but now they would have a little time to go over what had happened to her.

When Lacey stepped into the café, she wasn't alone. Dorran frowned at the sight of another woman with her. He hadn't realized Lacey would bring a friend, and he wasn't sure what to make of it. Maybe it would make her feel more comfortable, although Dorran hated the thought that he made anyone uncomfortable.

The friends were as different as they could be. Lacey was

blond and short, with warm brown eyes that lit up when she saw Dorran. The other woman was taller, possibly taller than Dorran, and had dark hair and eyes. Her expression was harsh, and she kept looking around as if she expected someone to jump them.

Dorran rose from his chair when Lacey came closer. "Hey," he said.

To his surprise, instead of waving at him or shaking his hand, Lacey stepped into his personal space and hugged him. His eyes widened, and he awkwardly patted her back. He didn't miss the way her friend glared at him, though, and he wondered what that was about. Maybe she thought Dorran was trying to seduce Lacey or something? It was laughable, but then, Dorran didn't know the woman, and she didn't know him.

"Thanks for coming," Lacey said as she stepped back. "This is Heather. She's my best friend, and she asked if I needed her support when I talked to you. I'm not sure I do, but I thought it couldn't hurt."

Dorran nodded at Heather, who didn't move toward him to shake his hand. That was fine with him. "Of course. Do you want to order something to eat before we start talking?"

"That's probably better."

They made small talk until their food arrived. Heather didn't participate much, and she still didn't look happy to be there, but then, who would be happy to talk about their best friend's stalker?

Once they settled down, Lacey looked at Dorran. "What do you need to know?"

"Everything you can remember, every single incident. I know you mentioned a few things when we talked on Friday, but has there been more?"

Lacey slowly nodded. "Well, I already told you about how I feel followed."

"Is that still happening?"

"Some days. I have to admit that I've been hiding in my apartment a lot, though. I mean, I still go to work, of course, but I've stopped going to the gym. I'm not comfortable being alone in the evening. I only go out when Austin is with me."

"I see." Dorran was pretty sure he would behave the same way he if he was in her shoes. "Anything else? You mentioned the flat tires and stuff disappearing from your apartment."

"There was also that letter," Heather said.

Dorran was surprised to hear her talk. "Letter?" he asked Lacey.

Lacey shrugged. "I found it inside my apartment. The letter was, well, let's just say it wasn't nice."

"Do you still have it?"

"No. I threw it away."

That was a pity. "Do you remember what was written in it?"

Lacey shook her head. "I never even fully read it. I freaked out when I realized what it was, and I threw it away."

"I can tell you if you want," Heather said.

That made Dorran frown. "You can?"

"I saw it. Lacey called me after she got it, and I went to her apartment. I took a peek, then threw it away again."

"Okay. If you could write down what it said, I can take a look at it with my boyfriend later. Lacey, you also mentioned being called at work?"

"Yeah, but even though I asked the receptionist about it, she couldn't tell me anything. The caller didn't give their name, and she said the voice was strange, as if whoever was talking had a sore throat or something."

Dorran didn't like any of this, but it looked like he was going to be neck-deep into it soon.

They continued talking, with Lacey telling him everything she'd gone through. Heather added a few things, obviously remembering them better than Lacey, which puzzled Dorran. He didn't think he would ever forget if something like this happened to him, but maybe he was wrong.

Dorran made a list, already going through it in his mind. He wasn't sure what to think about it or if there was anything to see. It probably pointed to someone, but Dorran couldn't see it.

"I don't know why Lacey thinks you can do anything," Heather said.

"What do you mean?" Dorran hoped he didn't come off as rude, even though he was mildly offended.

"You're not a police officer. You're *nothing*, not even a PI."

Lacey blushed. "Heather! You shouldn't talk to Dorran like that. He might not be a professional, but that doesn't mean he doesn't know what he's doing."

"How can he know what he's doing?"

"Do you not want me to help her?" Dorran asked.

Heather shook her head. "That's not what I was saying. I do think that Lacey is an idiot by talking to you rather than to someone who knows what they're doing. But I suppose it's better than nothing."

"You're right. My job has nothing to do with investigations. But my boyfriend is a police officer, and even though he can't do anything officially, he'll help me go over this. I also have been involved in more murders than I'm comfortable with, and I like to think that it's given me some insight into this kind of thing." He turned to Lacey. "But Heather is right. You should probably contact a professional, maybe a PI."

Lacey shook her head. "I don't want to."

"All right. I'll do what I can, and I'll keep you up to date." Dorran hesitated. He didn't want to do this, but he had to. "Do you have any idea if someone you know might be behind this? Maybe you can write me a list so I have their names."

After she'd asked for his help, he'd done some internet research on stalkers, and usually, the victims knew the people stalking them. That made sense, because Lacey's situation felt personal. Her apartment had been invaded, and her things had started disappearing. Whoever was stalking her knew her well enough to be able to walk in, do whatever they wanted, and leave, without Lacey noticing much of anything.

Dorran didn't like this, and he liked it even less once Lacey slid a piece of paper forward that she'd taken out of her purse so she could write. There was a short list of four names on it. He had four suspects, apparently.

"Can you tell me about them?"

Lacey shrugged. "I don't think any of them did anything."

"Still. You put them on the list for a reason. I'd just like to know what you're thinking. "Please."

"Fine. One is my father."

Dorran blinked at her. "Your father?"

"We have a bad relationship. He's misogynistic, homophobic, and in general, an asshole. I wouldn't be surprised if he did something like this, especially since he found out that Austin has Italian origins. He's a piece of shit, and he's also a racist. Then there's Bridget. She's one of my colleagues, and I got a promotion that she thought she should have had. She's been unpleasant since then. Sophie was one of my friends. We fought over something and lost contact. I think it's stupid for her to be on this list, but Heather thinks she might have something to do with it."

Dorran wrote all of this down next to the names. "And the last name? Tony?"

"He's my ex. I broke up with him because he cheated on me, and he tried to get me back. When I met Austin, he started getting menacing. He was never violent, and I truly don't think he's behind this, but Heather insisted in his case, too. Besides, he makes me uncomfortable enough that even though I don't think he has anything to do with it, I wouldn't be surprised if he did."

It looked like Dorran would have his work cut for him. He had four suspects, and while he agreed that for at least one or two of them, the chances they were the stalker were low, he would need to investigate all of them.

Dammit. He'd truly thought he was out of this, yet here he was, sticking his nose into business that wasn't his and probably putting his own life in danger once again.

Once home, Dorran spread his notes and the piece of paper Lacey had given him with the names on the coffee table. Then he went to grab his notepad and pen in his office. He couldn't avoid the coffee table, no matter how much he wanted to, so he decided to take the bull by the horns and went to sit on the couch, staring at his notes.

Okay. Where should he start? It wasn't the first time he'd done this, but this was different. In this case, no one had died, which was a good thing. It also meant it was harder, though. How was he supposed to find out which of these people were Lacey's stalker? If it was even one of them to begin with, of course.

He swallowed, then started going over his notes. In spite of the research he'd done, it was still hard to evaluate whether or not people he didn't know could do this. He only had their names, and he was starting to realize he would have to talk to the people if he wanted to be able to find out if one of them was coming after Lacey.

He grabbed the letter Heather had copied from memory. The tone was angry. The writer wanted Lacey to be aware of them and that they had something against her. Dorran glossed over the insults and tried to focus on what the letter said.

You don't deserve what you have.
It should have been mine.

I hate you.

"What are you doing?" Francis asked.

Dorran jumped, but he didn't say anything about it. It wasn't Francis' fault. "Trying to solve this case before someone gets hurt," he answered without looking away from the notes.

Francis appeared on the couch next to him and peered at the papers. "What's that?"

"You were here when Lacey and Austin explained why they wanted to talk to Eli and me, right?" Dorran didn't know for sure, but if he had to guess, it was a yes.

Francis nodded. "They're cute together," he said.

"They are, and they're worried."

Francis clicked his tongue. "I don't understand stalkers. Why would you want someone to be so afraid of you?"

Dorran didn't understand either. No matter how much he'd read about stalkers, he wasn't a psychiatrist, and he didn't understand them. He didn't have to, though. He just had to find this one.

"So," Francis said. "Where are you starting from.?"

Dorran rubbed his face. "I'm not sure, to be honest."

Francis leaned closer. He reached for the piece of paper with the names, but he couldn't take it, so he limited himself to dragging a finger along it. "A coworker? Really? Does Lacey think this woman would go after her because she got a promotion instead of her? Because I'm pretty sure that's one more reason for her *not* to be promoted in the first place."

He wasn't wrong. "I just asked her to write down every person she could think of that might be behind this. It doesn't mean the stalker is actually on the list, or that it's the coworker. I doubt it was her, or even Lacey's old friend, Sophie." But Dorran would need more details about that. Lacey had just said that she'd been friends with Sophie, but she hadn't explained why they weren't friends anymore, and that was probably important.

Dorran wrote that down, then went back to the list. "So you think we can take out the two women?"

Francis shrugged. "I don't know. We could take them out, but what will you do if it's one of them?"

"I'm pretty sure most stalkers are men, especially when the person being stalked is a woman." That tidbit of info had been on one of the websites he'd gone through.

"Most, sure. All of them, though? I don't think so."

Dorran groaned. "If I'd wanted to do this for a living, I would have. I'm a translator. Why would Lacey and Austin think that I would be good at this?"

Francis arched a brow. "Maybe because you've solved four murders?"

"But I had help. I talked to the ghosts of the victims. I can't talk to anyone in this case, though. No one died."

"I don't know how to help you. I wish I could."

"Thanks anyway." Dorran supposed it would be better to wait for Eli. He might not work this kind of case, but he was a detective, and he would know what he was doing.

Still, Dorran couldn't stay away from the notes. Instead of obsessing over finding who the stalker was, he decided to go on social media. He went on Sophie's profile first, poking around and trying to find out if it could be her. He didn't think so, especially since he found out the woman had moved to another city a few months before. It wasn't surprising that Lacey didn't know about it, since they weren't friends anymore, but it did take her off the list. If she wasn't even in town, she couldn't be stalking Lacey.

Dorran drew a line through her name, then moved on to the coworker.

Bridget was unhappy with the company she worked for, and she'd found another job and would start there in a couple of weeks. Dorran had no idea if it would be an improvement over the job she'd had before, but he supposed he could ask

Lacey about it, so he made a note about that, too. He didn't strike her off the list, just in case, but he doubted it was her.

That left him with the two men.

That was when Eli arrived home. Dorran heard the keys dangling and his footsteps in the hallway, and he smiled, relaxing against the couch and looking at the door.

When Eli came in, he smiled when he saw Dorran. "Hey," he said. "I wasn't sure I'd find you here." He took his jacket off and hung it, then unlaced his shoes and put them away. Then, he looked at Dorran, still grinning.

Dorran rolled his eyes. "You've done a good job putting your things away. Good man."

Eli groaned and shook his head. "Don't talk to me like I'm a kid." He moved closer and kissed the top of Dorran's head, then peeked at the coffee table. "What are you doing?"

Dorran sighed. "I met with Lacey for lunch. She gave me four names of people she thought could be her stalker, although of course, it can still be someone she doesn't know."

"Some stalkers don't know their victims, not personally. They build an entire story in their mind, but they don't talk to the people they're following, not in the beginning. Most stalkers are someone the victim knows, though, and the most common victim profile is that of a woman who had a previous intimate relationship with the stalker." Eli walked around the couch and came to sit next to Dorran. He took the list, then looked at Dorran. "Why is that name stricken out?"

"Because the woman moved a few months ago. Whatever happened between her and Lacey, I doubt she'd come back to do this."

"Okay. That does sound weird. I'll look into it, but you're probably right."

"What do you think about the coworker?" Dorran asked. "I'm pretty sure she got a new job, so I don't think it was her, either. I didn't want to strike her out, just in case."

Eli hummed as he went over Dorran's notes. "I don't think it was her. If she really got a new job, she wouldn't have a reason to. No matter how angry she was at Lacey, she got what she wanted in the end, so she wouldn't have a reason to do this." He tapped a fingertip on the piece of paper. "But you were right not to strike her out, just in case."

"Who do you think is doing it, then? Lacey's father, or her ex-boyfriend?"

"Well, exes are the first ones we look at in these cases. Since stalkers are more often men and have been close to the victim, it makes sense."

"That's what I was thinking, but again, I don't want to make assumptions. I think I need to talk to Lacey again, and this time, it would be better if she were alone."

Eli blinked. "She wasn't alone when you saw her today?"

"No. She brought a friend with her, which of course was fine, but Heather was kind of antagonizing. She made what she thought about me looking over this case obvious, and while I can't say I don't agree, it still wasn't nice."

Eli kissed Dorran's cheek. "You *can* do this. I know you can. But you shouldn't obsess over it. It's especially hard in this case because you know Lacey, and she might be in danger. But obsessing over everything won't help you. Take a break. Have dinner with me. We can look over your notes after dinner, once you've had the opportunity to think about something else and distract yourself."

He wasn't wrong. Dorran's instinct was to say no and to go back to the notes, but he doubted there was anything in them that he hadn't seen yet. He needed a break. "All right. What are you cooking for dinner?"

Eli laughed. "Are you sure you want to risk it?"

Dorran shook his head. "Chinese?"

Eli grinned. "Perfect."

CHAPTER SIX

The next time Dorran and Lacey met, Lacey was alone. Dorran breathed more easily and waved at her when she walked into the same café where they'd met two days before. She was on lunch break, which wasn't a problem for Dorran. Once again, he was grateful that he worked from home and made his own timetable. It was useful when he was investigating a stalker, even though that definitely wasn't his job.

Lacey came toward him. "Hi," she said, sounding breathless. "Sorry I'm late. I don't have a lot of time."

"That's okay," Dorran said, brushing her apology off. "I just wanted to go over your list again and ask if you remembered anything."

Lacey sat in the chair in front of Dorran. "Not really. I mean, I can't stop thinking about all of this, so I think I would remember if I missed something. What did you want to know about the list, though?"

Dorran explained to her that Sophie had moved away, while the other had found a new job. Lacey tsked when she heard about that second one. "I should have known. Of course she wouldn't just stay around when she didn't get that promotion."

"Is that a bad thing?"

"No. I mean, I never wished anything bad to happen to her. I'm happy I got the promotion, of course, but I did feel sorry that she didn't. It was just one promotion, though, you know? It was either her or me, but I'm grateful I got it. But knowing her, I'm not surprised that she found another job. She's resentful."

"Maybe, but since she *did* find another job, it doesn't make sense that she would stalk you, does it?"

"I don't know. I wouldn't have come to you and Eli if I'd figured out anything about this."

"You're not wrong, but I have to repeat that once again, I am not a professional. I honestly have no idea what I'm doing."

Lacey shook her head. "It's already more than what the police would do. So again, thank you. You've already eliminated at least one of the people on the list."

"I think we can take your colleague off, too. The only reason I haven't taken her off was that I wanted to make sure with you, but she's moving on, and from my research, stalkers are more likely to be males and someone you were once close to."

"Well, I haven't heard anything about the new job, but it's not surprising. It's not like we're friends or anything. I can't imagine she'd do something like that, but I thought I better put her on the list."

Dorran nodded. He still didn't strike out the name on the piece of paper, but he suspected he would be able to soon. "Are you sure there's no one else we can put on his list?" he asked.

"Of course not. I would have told you otherwise."

"What about Heather?" Dorran asked.

Lacey blinked. "Heather? I can't put her on the list. She's my best friend. She's always there for me, and she doesn't have a reason to do all of this."

Dorran raised his hands. "That's not what I meant." No matter how much he disliked Heather, she didn't fit the stalker profile. "I was just asking if she maybe had thought about someone else to put on the list."

Lacey's shoulders slumped. "Right. Sorry. I don't think she

has, though. She hasn't told me anything."

That was out, too. "I need to meet your father and your ex," he told Lacey.

"I wouldn't suggest you do that."

"But I have to if I want to make sense of the situation. I need to get to know them."

Lacey grimaced. "Better you than me, that's all I can say. I'm extremely grateful I won't ever have to see either of them again, to be honest."

"Can you tell me more about them? I'd like to be prepared when I see them." Especially since Lacey clearly disliked them.

She took the piece of paper from Dorran's hands, flipped it around, then took the pen Dorran had abandoned on the table while he was waiting for her and wrote down the addresses where he could find both her father and her ex. "You need to be careful, especially with my father. I already told you he's a dick, but you won't realize how much until you meet him. He's homophobic, so please, try not to mention Eli, at least not as your boyfriend. If you say you're there because of me, he's probably going to make fun of me, things like that. I honestly don't care what he has to say about me. I just need you to be careful."

Dorran tapped his fingertips on the table. "He's that bad?"

"He's probably worse than you can imagine."

Dorran had faced his fair share of horrible people, so he wasn't too worried except for one thing. "Is he violent?"

Lacey hesitated. "Well, he never hit my mother or me. Although, since they got divorced when I was a kid, maybe he just didn't have the opportunity to touch us. But as far as I know, he's not violent. I've never heard of him being in a fight or anything like that. *Still.* You have to be careful. Maybe you should ask Eli to go with you."

Dorran was tempted to do just that, but Eli was working.

Besides, Dorran was in charge of this, not his boyfriend, and he needed to do this alone, no matter how little he wanted to. He couldn't rely on Eli, not when Eli was busy. "I'll be careful," he promised.

"Please. I would never forgive myself if something happened to you because of me."

"But it wouldn't be because of you. It would be because of the stalker."

Lacey waved Dorran's words away. "You know what I mean. I asked you to get involved, and you agreed even though you didn't want to. I don't want anything to happen to you or to Eli."

"I'll be as careful as I can, but if you want me to find out who the stalker is, I have to do this."

Lacey leaned back in her chair. "Honestly? I'm not sure I want to find out who it is. I just want him to stop. I don't think I can deal with the fact that he could be my father or a man I once loved. I mean, I don't trust either of them, and I know they're assholes, but stalking me? That's taking it too far, or at least, I hope so."

Dorran hoped so for Lacey's sake, too, but if it wasn't either of those men, it meant it was someone she didn't know, and that would make it nearly impossible for him to find out who that person was.

He cleared his throat. "Are you still feeling followed?"

Lacey looked around as if she expected her stalker to jump out from behind one of the tables. "Sometimes. I try to be careful, but I have to follow a routine. I have to be at work in the morning, and I have to go home in the evening. So it hasn't been easy. I'm dealing with it, even though I hate it."

She shouldn't have to deal with this. "I'll do whatever I can," he promised.

She smiled at him. "I know. And I know I asked a lot of you. I'm grateful for the fact that you agreed, but don't beat yourself up if you never find out who the stalker is, as long as he stops. I know it's hard. I know it will be even harder if the stalker is someone I don't know. I still can't help but hope it is."

Dorran didn't know what to hope for except that he would come out of this alive and in one piece.

Dorran was not looking forward to meeting Bill, Lacey's father. He knew what to expect of the man, or at least, he hoped so. He would have no way to defend himself if Bill decided to attack him, so he hoped that wouldn't happen. Lacey had made it sound like he might, even though she'd said that her father had never been violent. Dorran wasn't sure if he could trust her on that, since she didn't have a lot of contact with him. Besides, Bill might not take it well if he was the stalker and Dorran started asking about it.

He looked at the small house he was parked in front of, took a deep breath, and got out. The door opened before he could even get to it, and a man stood there, glaring at him. "What do you want?" the man asked. He was in his late fifties, maybe early sixties. He wore jeans and a stretched-out t-shirt that had seen better days, and his gray hair was all over the place as if he'd been running his hand through it or he hadn't brushed it that morning. His stomach pushed out above his belt, and he gave it a good scratch as he watched Dorran.

Dorran rubbed the back of his neck, realized what he was doing, and straightened his back. "Hello, Mr. Owen. My name is Dorran. I'm a friend of your daughter."

Bill frowned. "Lacey?"

"Yes." Or did he have other daughters? Dorran hadn't thought to ask, which was probably a sign of how much he sucked at his job. He should know if Lacey had siblings, shouldn't he? "I was wondering if I could talk to you for a moment? It has to do with your daughter."

"Is Lacey okay?"

"She's perfectly fine, yes. But something's been happening to her, and I'd like to talk to you about it."

"You said you're a friend of hers?"

"I am." Dorran wasn't about to tell him that technically, he and Lacey were nearly in-laws. He didn't think bringing up Austin when Lacey had made it clear that her father didn't like him was a good idea.

Bill stared at him for a moment, then finally moved aside. Dorran stepped in and instantly wished he could go back out. The house smelled of cigarettes, and he felt his throat itch with the need to cough. Good thing he wasn't asthmatic. He forced himself to smile as he followed Bill into the kitchen. It was mostly clean, but the smoke seemed to cling to everything, including Dorran's skin, by this point.

"What's going on with her?" Bill asked, snatching a beer bottle from the table and taking a drink out of it.

Dorran cleared his throat, mostly because it was starting to ache. "Did you know that she has a stalker?"

Bill blinked. "A stalker?"

"Yes. Someone has been following her around and scaring her. From what she told me, that same person has also broken into her apartment and stolen things from her."

Bill's expression hardened. "And why are you telling me about this? You think I'm a stalker? That I would do this to my daughter?"

That was way too close for Dorran to be comfortable. "Of course not. I wanted to talk to you because you're Lacey's father, and I thought you might have some insight into this."

"Why are you asking those questions? Are you a cop?"

"I'm not. Unfortunately, the police wouldn't help Lacey. As long as nothing happens and she doesn't get hurt, they don't have a lot to work with. That's why she asked me to help her."

Bill snorted. "Are you sure she has a stalker? Because I wouldn't be surprised if she'd invented that. Or maybe it's that spaghetti-eater boyfriend of hers."

Dorran stiffened. He wasn't surprised by the insult, but he wished he hadn't had to hear it. "Her boyfriend doesn't have anything to do with it."

"Are you sure? He's not from here. His entire family is wrong. I wouldn't be surprised they had something to do with this, maybe that fag brother of his. Lacey told me about them, you know."

Dorran suspected Bill would think something was up if he continued to insist that Austin had nothing to do with it, or even worse if he snapped at him for the insults. It would be better to steer the conversation in another direction. "Stalkers are usually people who had a close relationship with the person they're after but aren't close to them anymore. This person managed to get into the apartment without Lacey noticing. That means they have a key."

Bill huffed. "And you want to know if I have one."

Dorran should have asked Lacey about this, but he supposed this was a better way. "I'm sure Lacey wouldn't have a problem answering that question, but since I'm here talking to you—"

Bill slammed the beer bottle onto the counter. "I don't have a key. She never gave me one, and I don't want one. Wouldn't want to stumble onto that guy she's dating. Besides, I'm sure she told you we're not close. She wouldn't give me a key. She doesn't even want to see me."

"Do you know anyone else who has a key? Maybe a friend, someone you think is weird, someone you don't quite trust."

"I already told you who I don't trust."

Lacey's boyfriend. Dorran trusted Austin implicitly, so he wasn't running for stalker of the year in Dorran's notes. He wasn't here for Austin anyway. He was here for Bill, but as rough as the man was, Dorran doubted he had the ability to be a stalker. He was more the kind of man who would yell at Lacey in the face rather than follow her around and steal things from her house. He was too blunt. He didn't have a problem telling Dorran what he thought, and Dorran didn't think things would be any different with his daughter.

Dorran didn't think Bill had anything to do with this. Still, since he was here, he might as well continue the conversation. "I already know Lacey's boyfriend has nothing to do with this. That's why I'm here. I wanted to ask you if you thought anyone in Lacey's past could be doing this. Maybe an old boyfriend? She doesn't want to believe anyone she knows would be capable of this, but I wouldn't be surprised."

Bill shook his head. "I haven't been in Lacey's life for a while. Her mother left me when she was a kid, and she took Lacey with her. I see her a few times a year, but no more, and I know almost nothing about her life. She only tells me about the important stuff, like when she graduated college and when she got with that boyfriend of hers. She wouldn't tell me about this. You're talking with the wrong person. You should be talking to her, not to me."

"I see. I just wanted to make sure you didn't have any information that could be useful. I'm not a professional, so anything I can find is a good thing."

Bill shook his head. "Tell that girl that she needs to go to the police, and if they won't do anything, she should buy a gun."

Dorran wasn't surprised that Bill would want to take care of this with firearms. "I'll relay the message." He reached into his pocket and took out one of his business cards. He'd made a bunch of them when he'd started translating, but he'd never needed them, so they were languishing in his closet. They came in handy in cases like these, though. "Will you please call me if you can think of anything? Even if it's only a minor detail. I'm walking in the dark here, and I need all the help I can get."

Bill snorted, but he took the business card. "Sure. Why not? But tell her to buy a gun. That's the best way to protect herself. She needs to shoot that fucker."

Dorran wouldn't relay that message. He wasn't sure what he'd gotten from the meeting, but it wasn't a lot, except for the conviction that Bill didn't have anything to do with the stalking.

That left only one name on Dorran's list — Tony, Lacey's ex. The man had taken it badly when she'd broken up with him, and even worse when she'd started dating Austin.

It wasn't going to be a fun meeting, either.

Dorran was exhausted by the time he got home, and he was relieved Eli was working late. That way he wouldn't have to cook for him.

But of course, things weren't that easy. When he got to his apartment, he found his best friend, Charlie, sitting in front of the door. He groaned, suddenly remembering why Charlie was there. "I forgot," he said as he reached his door.

Charlie rose to his feet and stretched. "I noticed. You didn't answer your phone."

"I'm sorry." Dorran hadn't told Charlie what he was doing yet, but obviously, the time had come. "Just give me a sec. I'm going to freshen up. Then we can go."

Charlie shook his head. "It's fine. It's obvious you're exhausted, and I don't want you to have to leave the apartment if you don't want to."

"I promised we'd go to dinner."

"We don't have to."

"But I *want* to." Dorran missed talking to his best friend. They'd both been so busy, Charlie with the wedding and Dorran with moving in with Eli and this freaking stalker thing.

He unlocked his door and slipped in, Charlie behind him. "I'll be right back," he said before disappearing into his bedroom.

He quickly washed up, changed his shirt, and when he went back to the living room, he found Charlie sitting down with Eli. He couldn't help the smile that bloomed on his face, and he made a beeline for his boyfriend. Eli tilted his head up and grinned at Dorran, and they kissed.

"Oh, my God. Is this what living together has done to you?" Charlie said. "I don't think I've ever seen Eli smile this much. You're going to get stuck that way, man."

Dorran chuckled and shook his head. "Shut it. You're the same with Theresa." He turned his attention back to Eli. "I promised Charlie we'd have dinner together."

"You can go, if you want, or maybe the three of us could go? Unless you two want some time alone."

Dorran looked at Charlie, who shrugged and shook his head. "You can come if you want. It's fine with me."

That was a relief. Dorran wanted his best friend and his boyfriend to get along. They headed out, and Dorran was once again relieved he wouldn't have to cook. He refused to let Eli cook, both because Eli was usually exhausted by the time he came home and because he'd probably poison them, but Dorran couldn't think of anything he wanted less than to spend time in the kitchen.

"Is everything okay?" Eli asked.

Dorran frowned. "Of course. Why are you asking?"

"Well, I know you were meeting Lacey today. You've also been quiet."

"It's hard to speak when Charlie's here. He never shuts his mouth." And sure enough, Charlie was chatting, mostly to himself, since Eli and Dorran were talking to each other. He didn't seem to care, though, as he talked about the newest video game he'd bought. He probably wouldn't be offended to find out Dorran and Eli weren't listening to him. He was just Charlie, exuberant and chatty, and he knew Dorran loved him, even when he wasn't listening to him.

Dorran shook his head. He didn't want to talk about the case in front of Charlie, even though he would have to mention it sooner or later. Right now, he wanted to forget everything about the stalker and Lacey, at least for a while. Meeting Bill had made him feel dirty, even though he didn't think Bill had anything to do with the case. He had to get all of that off his skin, and dinner was what he needed.

He leaned closer and kissed Eli. "We'll talk later, once we're back home, okay?"

Eli stared at him for a second, then nodded. "All right. But we *will* talk. It's obvious something's bothering you, and I don't like it."

Dorran couldn't help but smile at that. "You can't solve all the problems that bother me."

"Maybe not, but I can certainly try."

After that, it was easier to focus on dinner. Charlie hadn't even realized Dorran wasn't listening to him, and Dorran stepped into the conversation smoothly, asking him questions about the game and leaving Eli out. He knew Eli wouldn't mind. He wasn't a videogame kind of guy, and he knew Dorran and Charlie had some catching up to do.

And they did. "How's the wedding planning going?" Dorran asked.

Charlie groaned. "Please, can we not talk about that? I love Theresa, but she's becoming a bridezilla, and I don't know how to deal with that."

"That's because the wedding is coming closer. Think about it. This time next year, you'll be a married man."

Charlie paled. "Don't remind me of it."

"Why not? Please don't tell me you changed your mind."

"Of course not. I do wish we could do this with only us,

you know? I mean, I don't want to see my Great-uncle Jack. I don't care about him, and he probably doesn't care about me. Why should I invite him to the wedding? I only want the people I love and care for to be there, not the extended family I haven't seen in years."

"Then tell Theresa that. She loves you, and she'll understand."

It felt good to be talking about something that wasn't the stalker, and Dorran lost himself in the wedding planning, even though Charlie didn't want to talk about it. It was more than that. Dorran was trying to reassure his best friend that he was doing the right thing, and he was convinced that was the case. He'd always liked Theresa, and she was good for Charlie. They loved each other, and they would be great together. They already were. Dorran understood why Charlie was freaking out, but he didn't think he had a good reason.

He was still relaxed once he and Eli headed home after saying goodbye to Charlie. He hummed as they walked and smiled when Eli took his hand. Eli wasn't crazy about PDA, but he was starting to be more relaxed, and in turn, Dorran was, too. The fact that he was full of good food and a bit of wine probably helped, too.

"How are you feeling?" Eli asked.

"Great. I needed this."

"You should do it more often."

"I wish I could, but it's hard. Both Charlie and I have a lot of things to take care of, and it's hard to find time to see each other. We're not college kids anymore. We're both adults." And they didn't live together anymore.

"Want to talk about the stalker?"

Dorran sighed. "Not particularly, but I guess."

Still, he waited until they were home, flopped on the couch, with his head against Eli's shoulder. "I met Lacey's father today," he explained.

"And?" Eli asked when Dorran didn't continue.

"The guy is a dick. I'm not going to repeat what he said, but I wanted to throttle him after only a few seconds. Lacey wasn't kidding when she said he was an asshole."

"A stalker asshole?"

Dorran hesitated, then shook his head. "I don't think so. He's blunt. He doesn't have a problem telling you exactly what he thinks about you to your face. I don't see him as a stalker. He's just not the type."

Eli rubbed a hand on Dorran's side. "I'm sorry I'm not helping more. I said I would, and I disappeared."

"You don't have to apologize." Eli had a new case, and he was working on that. It was more important than helping Lacey, and it was his job.

"I do. I feel like you wouldn't have agreed to help Lacey if I hadn't pushed you into it, and I did so only because I wanted to help you. I was planning to. It's just that—"

"The new case. I know."

Eli kissed the top of Dorran's head. "Follow your instincts. I know you don't think you can trust them, but you can. If you don't think Lacey's father had something to do with this, then he probably didn't. Focus on your other suspects. Think about everyone and everything. You'll find out who the stalker is. I have faith in you."

Dorran wasn't so sure, but he couldn't get out of it, not anymore. He needed to help Lacey before something happened to her. He couldn't be sure the stalker's behavior would worsen, but what would be the odds that it didn't? Dorran didn't like thinking about Lacey being in danger, and he wasn't going back on his word.

He had to help, even though he didn't know if he could.

CHAPTER SEVEN

After what had happened with Lacey's father, Dorran couldn't say he was looking forward to talking with Tony, Lacey's ex. She'd been more specific when she'd warned Dorran about her father, but that didn't mean Tony wasn't just as bad. Lacey had said something about him cheating on her and not taking it well when she broke up with him, so Dorran was ready for just about anything to happen.

He wasn't ready for Tony himself, though.

They met in a coffee shop, mostly because Dorran wasn't about to do this in a place where he and Tony would be alone. He hadn't feared for his life when he'd met Lacey's father, but he'd realized later that it had been stupid to meet him on his own. What if he'd been the stalker and if he'd decided to shut Dorran up for finding out? Dorran wasn't going to risk that a second time, even though he wasn't looking forward to talking to Tony where people could hear them. It was what it was, though.

But when Tony came in, he looked almost happy. Dorran had only mentioned that he was one of Lacey's friends, and he wasn't sure what Tony thought that meant. Maybe that Lacey had sent Dorran because she wanted to get back with him?

Dorran could see why Lacey had been interested in Tony, at least physically. He was tall, and his curly dark hair fell in front of his forehead. He pushed a curl away, then sat in front of Dorran and grinned at him. "Hey, man. I'm Tony."

Dorran blinked. "I'm Dorran."

"That's a nice name."

Dorran blinked. "Thank you." He wasn't quite sure what to say. "And thank you for coming."

Toby shrugged one muscled shoulder. "No worry. When you said it was about Lacey, I knew I had to come. How's she doing?"

Dorran had to be careful. If Tony was the stalker, he didn't want him to think he suspected him. "She's doing okay, but she does have a big problem, and she asked me to look into it."

Tony frowned. "A problem?" He sounded like this wasn't what he'd expected, which reinforced Dorran's opinion that maybe he'd thought that Lacey wanted to get back with him.

Dorran cleared his throat. "Yes. She told me about you."

Tony's smile widened. "She did? I hope it was all good things. We had a good time together."

"I'm sure you did, but she mentioned how you took it when she broke up with you, and when she met her current boyfriend."

The transformation was stunning. The smile disappeared from Tony's lips, and his expression hardened. Dorran looked around, relieved he'd chosen to do this here with a few people around. He didn't think Tony was about to beat him up — yet. It was a strong possibility, though, considering Tony's body language.

"What did she tell you?" Tony asked, and his voice was even harsher than his expression.

"Well, she said that you didn't take it well."

"She dumped me. Of course I didn't take it well. What the fuck do you want?"

"Just to talk to you. And it has nothing to do with your break-up." Just like with Bill, Dorran wasn't about to tell him he suspected Tony could be Lacey's stalker.

"She treated me like shit. Why should I help her?"

"Her life might be in danger."

That seemed to get through to Tony. "What do you mean?"

Dorran had to choose his words carefully. "Someone's been stalking her," he finally said.

Tony blinked at him. "A stalker?"

"That's what I said, yes."

"Let me guess. You think *I'm* the stalker."

Dorran wasn't sure what to think about Tony's tone. He didn't sound as angry as before, but Dorran doubted he was happy about this. "That's not what I said."

"She sent you to make sure I wasn't the stalker, though, didn't she? Who are you? A cop?"

The situation was unraveling fast. "I'm not a cop. I'm just Lacey's friend, and she never said you were the stalker. When she said she was with you for a while, I thought I could talk to you to ask you if you have any idea of who the stalker might be."

Tony looked suspicious, but he wasn't storming out, so that was a good thing. "You think I can help you?"

"I hope you can. Can you think of anyone who might do this to Lacey?"

"Of course not. And I have nothing to do with it. I don't care about her anymore. I'm over her."

Dorran nodded, even though it was pretty obvious that Tony was anything but. "Of course. How about her father? Did you ever meet him?"

Tony snorted. "Yeah, I did. He was an okay guy. A bit rough around the edges, but I don't think he would do something like this. He's not smart enough, you know?"

Dorran didn't, but he still made a note in his notebook. "Anyone else? Lacey hasn't been able to give me more than a few names, and I'm not sure where to begin."

"Shouldn't you go to the police?"

"She did, but they can't do anything until something

58

happens. So far, she's been followed, and someone's written her a nasty letter, then called her a few times and hung up when she answered. But she's scared, and I'm afraid that the stalker will escalate if we don't do anything."

Toby shook his head and got to his feet. "Look, I'm sorry for what Lacey's going through. She might have been a bitch to me, but she doesn't deserve to be scared like this. But I have nothing to do with it, and I don't know how to help you. I don't think it was her father, but he was a bit of a dick, so maybe you should look into him. But I've moved on. Lacey is part of my past, not my future." He hesitated. "But let me know if something happens, okay?"

"I thought she was part of your past."

"She is. That doesn't mean I don't care about her. We might not have parted the best way, but I loved her once. I don't want anything to happen to her."

Dorran nodded, and Tony took it as a goodbye. He turned around and left without adding anything, leaving Dorran sitting at his table with his coffee.

Dorran wrapped his hands around the mug, letting the warmth seep into his skin. That had gone better than expected, but he still had no idea who the stalker was. He'd thought it could be Tony, but now, he wasn't so sure. He also wasn't sure it was Bill. Bill didn't fit the profile of most stalkers, while Tony did. Of course, everything Tony had told him could be fake. Maybe he wasn't over Lacey. Maybe he still loved her and was angry at her for dumping him and getting with Austin. How was Dorran supposed to find out about that, though? He couldn't follow Tony around. He might be able to look into his life, but he could only use social media, and it probably wouldn't be as useful as he hoped.

He needed to talk to Eli. He would know what to do, and he had more resources. It was his job after all, even though Dorran was doing it.

CHAPTER EIGHT

Dorran still wasn't used to the phone ringing in the middle of the night. He jerked up when he heard it, blindly looking around, wondering what was happening. A hand on his chest pushed him back. "It's probably work," Eli murmured.

Right. Work. Because Eli was a cop, and it wasn't strange for him to get a phone call in the middle of the night.

Dorran's heart was racing, but he stretched out again, closed his eyes, and tried to go back to sleep. If it was work, then Eli would soon leave, and Dorran would be able to sleep a few more hours at the very least. It was still dark, so it had to be early in the morning.

He didn't like those phone calls, but he understood they were necessary. He'd known what Eli's job was when he'd started dating him, and when they'd moved in together. He'd expected this to happen. He didn't like it, but he also wasn't going to bust Eli's balls about it. His guy was a detective, and Dorran had to live with it.

"Calm down," Eli murmured. "What's going on? Tell me."

Dorran frowned and rolled toward Eli. It didn't sound like a work call, but he wasn't sure yet. He wouldn't be sure until Eli said something, and so far, he was focused on the caller. "Austin, you have to calm down," Eli repeated, and through the words, Dorran could hear the hint of panic in Eli's voice. He sat up and touched Eli's shoulder to tell him that he was there for him if he needed him. Eli gave him a grateful smile, but his focus was still on the phone. "Where is she?" he asked.

Dorran wanted to hear what Austin was saying, but he

60

couldn't. The only thing he could do was to wait, and he hated it. Were they talking about their mother? Or about Lacey? Dorran had no way to know, and he didn't like not knowing.

"Okay. Do you want us to come to the hospital?" Eli asked. Dorran was ready to get up, but Eli grabbed his wrist and pulled him back into bed. "All right. Well, we're here if you need us. Call if you need anything, and I'm serious, Austin. This isn't a small thing. She was attacked. What did the officers who intervened say?"

Shit. It was Lacey, and she'd been attacked. Dorran had no doubt that the culprit was her stalker, and a wave of guilt threatened to push him down. He hadn't done enough. He knew it wasn't his job, but he'd agreed to help Lacey, and instead, she'd been hurt. How was he supposed to deal with that? Hell, how was *Lacey* supposed to deal with it? She was the one in danger.

"I'll call you tomorrow," Eli said. "I know it's useless to say this, but try to get some sleep after you're sure Lacey's fine. Staying awake the entire night won't help either you or her. And let me know if anything else happens. I'm not kidding, Austin."

He hung up a few seconds later, and Dorran looked at him. "What happened?"

Eli sighed, and his shoulders slumped. "Lacey was attacked on her way home from a night out. Austin didn't give me any details. I don't think he could, not with how frantic he sounded. But he said enough that I know Lacey will be okay. She was just scratched, and while she was taken to the hospital, it was mostly because the police wanted pictures for the report."

"They're finally involved?"

"Looks like it. I mean, they can't ignore this anymore, not when Lacey was attacked. It doesn't mean they're going to be able to do anything, though."

Dorran nodded. "I was the one who was supposed to do something."

Eli wrapped an arm around Dorran's shoulders and pulled him back down to the bed.

There was nothing Dorran wanted less than to go back to sleep, but he settled against Eli's chest and allowed his boyfriend to comfort him.

"You've done everything you could," Eli said. "Haven't you?"

"Of course I have. But you know this isn't my job. I have no idea what I'm doing."

"Yet you still agreed to help. I'm sure Lacey and Austin are grateful for that. Don't beat yourself up, Dorran. You had nothing to do with this. It would have happened even if you hadn't looked into it."

Dorran wasn't too sure about that. "What if me talking to Lacey's father and her ex triggered this? What if one of them is the stalker and decided to take another step because of the conversation I had with him?"

Eli took a moment to answer, and Dorran held his breath. "I don't think that's the case, but I can't promise you it's not. This stalker is escalating, and he could have been triggered by your conversation or by something else. We can't know until we know who he is. That doesn't mean that's the case, though. It could be that one of them is the stalker and they decided to up the ante because of the way Lacey's been behaving. Even though you talked to them, she's the one who started this. I don't know what the stalker has in mind, but it's not going to be good. It was going to escalate anyway, whether or not you talked to him."

"And if it isn't one of the two guys I talked to?" Dorran suspected Tony, but how could he be sure? It fit with everything, but he wasn't about to tell Eli he thought Tony had done it, not when there was a chance that Tony was innocent.

"Then I have no idea what pushed the stalker to escalate, but again, it's always hard to say in these cases. The only thing we know for sure is that Lacey needs to be protected. She was lucky tonight, but she might not be next time."

"You think there'll be a next time?"

"There is always a next time, unfortunately. I wish I could do more, but honestly, I'm glad I'm not involved, not professionally."

Because if Eli were, it would mean that Lacey was dead. "She's going to be okay, isn't she?"

"Tonight, yes. For the rest, I don't know. I don't want to make promises that might not be true."

"I know."

"Try to go to sleep. Austin didn't want us to go to the hospital. He's pretty sure they're going to go home soon anyway. I don't think he'll call again tonight, so we should get some rest. Tomorrow's going to be a mess."

Dorran nodded and closed his eyes, but he already knew it would be hard for him to go to sleep.

It might not have been his fault, but could he really ignore the possibility that it was? He hadn't been the one who'd attacked Lacey, but he'd stuck his nose into the situation, and he might have caused it. What if Lacey had been killed? Would he have been able to live with himself then?

He didn't know, and he hoped he would never have to find out. Things were getting worse, and that was probably because of how bad he was at this. It truly wasn't his job, and he needed to stop. If there was even one chance that his words had triggered the attack, it was one too many. It was over, and he was going to tell Eli and everyone else exactly that.

Tomorrow, though. Tomorrow, Dorran would call Lacey and ask her how she was. He'd make sure she was okay. Then he would tell her that he wasn't going to continue investigating anymore. Now that she'd been attacked, it was more serious, and the police would have to take care of it.

Still, Dorran had a hard time stopping his brain from going over every detail he'd gathered in the few days he'd been looking into this. Who was the stalker? Was it Bill or Tony? Or was it someone else entirely?

CHAPTER NINE

Dorran had tried to work, but he couldn't focus. His day was shot, and he'd stopped trying after a while. Eli had gotten a phone call from Austin early in the morning, telling him that both he and Lacey were okay and that they were back at her apartment. Eli had gone to work after that, leaving Dorran alone with his thoughts.

That wasn't a good thing, not this time.

Dorran hadn't been able to forget what had happened, and he needed to do something. What, though? He hadn't heard from Lacey again, and he probably wouldn't. She had to realize that he couldn't do this anymore, not when things were getting this bad. Still, he wished Lacey had let him know she was okay. They weren't friends, exactly, but they were something. Not family, not yet, but eventually. That had to mean something, didn't it?

When Dorran's phone rang, he rushed to get it, grabbing it and looking at the screen. He smiled in relief when he saw Lacey's name flash on the screen and answered. "Lacey. Austin told us what happened. How are you?"

"Dorran? I need you. I need help."

There was so much panic in Lacey's voice that it got Dorran's attention right away. "What happened?" Was it the stalker again?

"Austin went to the grocery store. Tony is here. I don't know what to do. He tried to get in, and I managed to close the door, but he's still out there, and he's pounding on my door, and I don't know what to do." She sobbed. "Please,

Dorran."

"Have you called Austin yet?"

"I tried, but he didn't answer."

"All right." Dorran was already moving, putting his shoes on and taking his keys from the hook in the entrance. "Call him again. He's probably closest to you. I'm going to call Eli on my way to your apartment." Wait. He didn't have her address. "You need to text me your address before calling Austin, though."

"I'll do it. Please. I can't be here alone, not with Tony doing this."

"I'll be there soon as I can. I promise." Now that he knew what was happening, Dorran could hear Tony pounding on the door and yelling at Lacey. He hated that she had to go through this. "Go as far away from the door as you can. It's locked, right?"

"Yeah. I locked it as soon as I closed it."

"Good. Then go to the bedroom or the bathroom. Lock yourself in if you can." Hopefully, if Tony was trying to hurt her, that would at least slow him down enough that Dorran or Austin would get there before he could do anything.

Dorran wasn't sure what he would do if he got there first. He wasn't a fighter. It wasn't his job. He might get hurt, but he couldn't abandon Lacey, and it wouldn't be the first time he got hurt anyway. He was getting used to it.

"I'm scared," she murmured.

Dorran was scared, too, but he wasn't going to tell her that. "Call Austin. If he doesn't answer, call me again, and I'll stay on the phone with you until I get there, all right?"

"All right."

Dorran didn't waste time. As soon as Lacey hung up, he called Eli. He prayed his boyfriend would answer and that he wasn't interrogating a suspect or hunting down a murderer. He almost slumped with relief when Eli's voice came through the phone. "Dorran?"

"Eli. There's a problem. Tony is at Lacey's apartment, and he's pounding on the door and trying to get in."

"Shit. How do you know?"

"She called me. She tried to call your brother, but he didn't answer."

"I thought they'd both taken the day off."

"She said he went grocery shopping. I told her to try calling him again, but if he doesn't answer this time, either, she'll call me back. I need to hang up. You know where she lives?"

"Yeah. I asked Austin to give me her address and phone number, just in case."

"I'm going."

"You can't. What if Tony is the stalker? What if he gets violent?"

Dorran was terrified, and he wanted to stay home. He couldn't, though. "I promise I'll be careful. I won't try to talk to him or to antagonize him. I need to go, though." Because Lacey had called him. Because she trusted him to protect her. Dorran didn't know what he'd done to earn that trust, but he wasn't going to betray it.

"I'm not going to be able to stop you, am I?" Eli asked.

"No. I need to go."

"Be safe. Please."

Dorran didn't have the time to be surprised that Eli wasn't ordering him to stay home. He hung up the phone and rushed to his car. He had to try a few times to get the key in the ignition because of how hard his hand trembled. He needed to calm down, so he forced himself to stop and take a few deep breaths.

He was wasting time, but he needed it. He wouldn't help anyone if he crashed the car on his way to Lacey's apartment.

Once he felt better, he started the car and headed out. Lacey had texted him her address, but she hadn't called back, so hopefully, she'd managed to get Austin to answer. Dorran wasn't sure whether that was a good thing. He didn't know Austin well, but he could imagine how the man would react at finding his girlfriend's ex-boyfriend terrorizing her. It wouldn't end well if Dorran didn't get there first.

But he was too late. When he got to Lacey's building, he climbed the stairs instead of using the elevator. It was probably a bad decision considering how out of breath he was when he got to Lacey's floor, but when he opened the stair door and stepped into the hallway, he could hear the voices.

Austin had already come back, and he and Tony were fighting. Dorran rushed toward the sounds, sucking in a breath when he saw the situation that he was walking in on.

Lacey's door was open, and she was standing there, her hands covering her mouth, her eyes wide. Tears slid down her cheeks as she watched her boyfriend and her ex-boyfriend trying to hit each other in the hallway.

Austin was holding his own, but Tony was more muscled and taller. Dorran knew it wasn't going to end well for him if he intervened, but he had to at least attempt to separate them.

He ran toward them. "Austin! Stop it. You're scaring Lacey. Both of you are."

They didn't even look at him, and he might as well not have said anything for all the reaction he got. He didn't know where to start when it came to separating two guys punching each other, but he had to try. When he saw Austin cock his hand back to punch Tony in the face, he grabbed his wrist. Austin jerked back and looked at him, his face pale and his eyes wide. "Let me go," he snapped, trying to pull his arm away.

Dorran didn't let go, or at least, he didn't let go until Tony's fist hit his face.

Pain exploded around his eye, and he tumbled back. He

reached out, covering his face with his hand.

"Shit, Dorran," Austin said, but Tony wasn't done with him, and he had to duck to avoid another punch.

Dorran sucked at fighting, and he needed to stay out of it. Luckily for him, the cavalry arrived. The elevator doors opened, and Eli and Mel rushed out. Once they were there, everything slowed down. Tony seemed to realize they were police officers, and he stopped trying to punch Austin. He pressed his back against the wall and raised his hands as if Eli and Mel might shoot him. They didn't even have their guns out, but Dorran could understand that instinct. "I didn't do anything," he said. "I saw Lacey was attacked on social media, and I wanted to check in on her. That's all."

Mel shook his head and went to take care of Tony — hopefully to arrest him — while Eli focused on Austin and Dorran. "How are you doing?"

Dorran let go of his face, even though his eye felt like it was on fire. "Not sure. How bad is it?"

Eli looked at him and swore. "What happened to you?"

"I got punched trying to separate them."

Eli gently cradled Dorran's face with his hands and turned it this way and that to get a better look. "How much does it hurt?"

"I'll live." Eli didn't look convinced, so Dorran forced himself to smile, even though doing so hurt, too. "I promise. I'm fine. It hurts a bit, and I have to say I'm not looking forward to getting punched again if this is how much it hurts, but I'll be fine. Take care of Tony. Take him away from here. Lacey is terrified."

Austin had left their side as soon as he'd seen Dorran was in good hands, and he was with Lacey, his arms wrapped around her. He was stroking her hair and murmuring to her, and Dorran felt better. He might have gotten punched in the process, and he might not have done much, but everyone was okay.

"I have to go," Eli said.

"I know. Don't worry about me. Do your job. I'll be fine."

"Call me as soon as you're home, okay?"

"I will. I think I'm going to stay here for a while to make sure Lacey's okay, but I'll text you when I leave, and I'll call you when I'm home."

Eli clearly didn't want to go, but he had to. As soon as he left, Austin moved to Dorran. "I'm really sorry about your eye," he said.

Dorran shook his head. "I'm fine." Was anyone going to believe him?

"Why don't you come in? I can find some ice for you. You can sit down for a bit before going home."

"Thank you." Dorran had been trying to show he was strong, but even though it had only been a punch, he was shaken.

"I wanted to thank you," Austin said as they stepped into the apartment. "I know Lacey called you when she couldn't get me. You helped her with this and with the stalker thing. I'm so relieved it's over now."

Dorran blinked, and damn, that hurt. "Over?"

"Well, I don't know if Tony is going to get arrested for the stalking, since the cops couldn't do anything before this, but we're sure as hell going to press charges. Hopefully, after what just happened, he'll stay away from Lacey and stop stalking her."

Dorran nodded, but he wasn't convinced. If Tony was the stalker, he'd been smart until now. He'd moved in the shadows, so much that no one had known for sure if he was the stalker. Even when he'd attacked Lacey the night before, no one had recognized him, not even Lacey. Why had he changed the way he behaved? Why had he decided to come and talk to Lacey face to face? It didn't make sense, but maybe it was only because Dorran's brain still hurt from that punch.

CHAPTER TEN

For once, Dorran was looking forward to Sunday lunch with Eli's family. He wanted to check in on Lacey and Austin and make sure they were okay after what had happened with Tony.

That situation was a mess. Eli hadn't gone into details, but since Tony had been caught in the act of assaulting Austin and he'd threatened Lacey, he was going to be charged with assault. Dorran didn't know what would happen to him, but he knew better than to hope he would get jail time. Besides, he might deserve it, but that didn't mean the stalker situation was resolved.

He'd had time to think about it. Even though he hadn't talked with Eli, he still didn't understand why Tony would have changed his behavior so much if he was the stalker, and he didn't feel right about the situation. Tony deserved to go to jail, or at least to pay for assaulting Austin and scaring Lacey to death, but he didn't deserve to pay for something he hadn't done if he wasn't the stalker.

Was he, then? Dorran didn't know the answer to that question. He didn't know where to start. Because of that, he decided to stop thinking about it for the day, or if he couldn't for an entire day, at least long enough to have lunch with Eli's family.

The house was familiar to Dorran now. He smiled as they walked in, inhaling the scents of the delicious food Eli's mother was cooking. She came to find them only seconds after they'd said hello to the rest of the family. She opened her arms and pulled Eli into a bear hug. "How are you? Austin told us everything that happened. Are you okay?"

Eli patted her back. "I'm fine. I did nothing except arrest the asshole. Austin and Dorran kept him occupied until we got there."

She turned her attention to Dorran, and to his surprise, she pulled him closer, wrapping her arms around him, too. He wasn't quite sure how to respond, so he awkwardly patted her back the same way Eli had. "You saved them," she said.

"I didn't do anything. I just distracted Tony for a few minutes."

She pushed him back, but she didn't let go of him, holding him at arm's length as she looked him over. Her gaze flickered to his black eye, and she grimaced. "You obviously did more than distracting him for a few minutes. You were there when Lacey called you and when my boy needed you. Thank you."

Dorran shook his head. "You have nothing to thank me for. Anyone would have done the same."

She clicked her tongue. "I'm going to get some ice for your eye."

"I don't think it's necessary. It's been a few days now. The swelling is coming down."

She ignored Dorran's protests. "Sit. I'll be right back."

Eli chuckled as his mother stepped away. "You know you won't be able to convince her to let this go, right? You might as well go along with it and obey."

Dorran wasn't used to being fussed over, but he knew Eli was right. His mother wouldn't take no for an answer, so he sat on the couch. He was grateful no one asked him about his eye, although he realized it was because they already knew what had happened.

"What did you tell her?" he asked Eli.

"Nothing. Austin beat me to it. He and Lacey apparently called my mom the day after it happened and told her how heroic you were."

Dorran's cheeks heated. "I'm not a hero. I didn't do any-thing."

Eli patted his knee. "You were there when Lacey needed you. That's more than a lot of people would have done, no matter what you try to convince yourself of. You barely know her, yet you went to her apartment even though you knew it could end badly for you."

"Anyone would have done it," Dorran insisted. He wasn't special.

"I'm not too sure about that, Dorran. I've seen a lot of things in my job, and I know a lot of people would have turned around and looked the other way because it wasn't their business. You didn't."

Maybe so, but it still made Dorran uncomfortable. He was grateful when Eli stopped talking about it and turned to speak to his father, and even though he knew he shouldn't, he let his thoughts drift to Tony.

Maybe he should ask Eli what was going on with the man. He doubted he was still at the station, which meant he was free. Was he still stalking Lacey? Or maybe he wasn't the stalker. Maybe he had nothing to do with it.

How was Dorran supposed to find out, though? He could try talking to Tony again, but he doubted the man would al-low him anywhere close to him. Besides, he didn't want to risk it. He'd been punched once already. Would Tony hit him again if he tried to talk to him? He probably associated Dorran with Lacey and Austin and the police now.

"What are you thinking about so hard?" Eli asked, startling Dorran.

"What?"

Eli narrowed his eyes. "What are you thinking about? It's obvious you're not listening to the conversations. Are you un-comfortable? Do you want to go home? Are you in pain?"

Dorran shook his head. "I'm fine. I was fine yesterday, and I'm fine today. I promise."

"There's something, though."

Eli wasn't a detective for nothing. Dorran wasn't going to lie to him. "There is something, yes. And I'd like to talk to you about it." He couldn't help but wonder what Eli would think about the possibility that Tony wasn't the stalker. Austin and Lacey hoped it was him and that everything was over, but Eli would look at the case without prejudice.

Eli stared at Dorran for a second, then nodded. "As long as you're sure it can wait."

"I promise it can." Dorran was making a lot of promises for later, but that was okay. "We'll talk once we're home, okay?"

"All right. We'll talk at home."

It was easier to focus on Eli's family after that. Dorran had doubts, and he didn't want Tony to pay for something he possibly hadn't done, but this wasn't his job. Besides, he might be wrong, and if Tony was the stalker, then he deserved to do jail time.

Eli might have news about Tony, maybe more details to give Dorran. Hopefully, if they put their heads together, they would be able to solve this.

Or at least, Dorran hoped so. He was less and less convinced that Tony had anything to do with the stalking, and he felt guilty. He might not have pointed his finger at Tony, but he'd still insinuated the man could be the stalker, and he didn't want to be the reason Tony lost his freedom if he didn't deserve it.

Francis was waiting for them when Eli and Dorran got home. Dorran barely had the time to take his shoes off before the ghost was standing there with his arms crossed over his chest. "How did it go?" he asked.

Dorran frowned. "It was lunch. How do you think it

went?"

Francis grinned. "You're a hero. Did they fawn over you?"

Dorran glared. He wasn't surprised Francis knew what had happened. Hell, Dorran had been the one to explain, at least in part. He hadn't been able to avoid it, considering he had a black eye. He was surprised to know that Eli and Francis had talked, but maybe he shouldn't be. Right now, Eli wasn't telling Francis to leave, and he wasn't trying to ignore him, either. He behaved as if Francis was an annoying roommate, smiling at him when he passed by him on his way to the living room.

It was a huge change. Until recently, Eli had denied ghosts existed and that Dorran could see them. Even after he'd seen the proof that he was wrong, he'd had a hard time wrapping his mind around it. Dorran wasn't convinced he had, not entirely, but from the way Eli was behaving, maybe Dorran was wrong.

"I'm not a hero," Dorran grumbled.

"Sure you are. You saved Lacey and Austin, didn't you? You found Lacey's stalker?"

Dorran hesitated. He wanted to say yes to that, but he wasn't sure he could. Of course, Eli noticed his hesitation. He sat on the couch and patted it, silently asking Dorran to sit with him. Dorran obeyed. He snuggled against Eli's side, smiling when Eli wrapped his arms around him.

"So?" he asked. "You said we would talk once home."

"I'd hoped you would give me more than a few seconds, but yeah. Okay. Let's talk." Dorran straightened. He turned around on the couch, pulling his legs under himself. He faced Eli and tried to find a way to explain how he felt and what he thought without telling Eli that he believed the police would be botching their investigation if they arrested Tony for being Lacey's stalker.

"Are your colleagues still looking into this stalker thing?"

he asked.

Eli blinked. "They are. I trust them, so you don't have to worry about that. It's not your job anymore. You did everything you could. Now, it's out of your hands."

"They think it was Tony after what Tony did?"

"I don't know. I haven't talked to them. My brother is involved, so it wouldn't be right."

"Did they suspect him?"

"I think so. I mean, Tony's behavior wasn't exactly normal. Everything does seem to point to the fact that he *is* the stalker."

Dorran couldn't deny that it could be him. He didn't have a lot of suspects, and from what he knew about stalkers, Tony did fit the bill. He was Lacey's ex, so they'd had an intimate relationship. He hadn't taken their break-up well. He was angry at her for being with Austin and dumping him. Besides, all the other suspects on Dorran's list didn't make much sense. The two women might have been angry with Lacey, but it wasn't a good enough reason to stalk her. Lacey's father, well, while he might fit part of the bill, he wasn't subtle enough to do something like that. He was the kind of man who told you what he thought about you to your face, which Dorran suspected he had done more than once considering what Lacey had told him about her father. That didn't point to a stalker.

Eli reached for Dorran again. He pulled him closer, then kissed the top of his head. "I know you're worried. I am, too. I hate that this happened to Lacey and Austin, but it's over. You don't have to worry about them anymore. Tony is under investigation, and I'm sure that if he is the stalker, my colleagues will find out and they'll make sure he pays."

"I'm just not sure he's a stalker, and I don't want him to pay for something he didn't do."

Eli hesitated. "I know I told you to trust your instincts, and

I'm not changing my mind. If you think he might not have had anything to do with the stalking, then that's a possibility. But you're not a cop, Dorran. This isn't your job, and I shouldn't have pushed you to agree to this. You got hurt, and that's entirely on me."

Dorran shook his head. "I didn't get hurt. I got punched. It's not that bad."

"Maybe, but still, I hate looking at you and seeing that bruise. I know I wasn't the one to put it there, but I contributed. I won't push you again, especially when you were so uncomfortable to do this in the first place. I'm sorry."

"You might have pushed me, but I would probably have agreed anyway. I wanted to help Lacey." And he still did. He just didn't know if he could. He didn't think there was anything he could do.

"Just let it go," Eli murmured. "If the stalker isn't Tony, then the police will find out. They know that Austin is my brother, so they're giving this all their attention. It might take a while, because stalker cases are never easy to deal with, but it's their job."

He was right. There was nothing Dorran could do, and he needed to relax and let it go. Even if Tony wasn't the stalker, Eli's colleagues would find out, and hopefully, they would find the real stalker.

But the doubts were still there. Dorran couldn't ignore them, no matter how much he wanted to. If Tony wasn't the stalker, who was? Stalkers were usually someone who had an intimate relationship with their victim, but none of the people on the list had that except for Tony and Lacey's father, and Dorran didn't think either of them was the stalker. That left two women, but they didn't make sense, either.

So who was the stalker? Was there someone else that Dorran hadn't looked into? Someone Lacey couldn't believe would be the stalker, so she hadn't put them on the list? Was the stalker someone Lacey didn't know?

Dorran had no idea, and he didn't know if he would ever be able to find out. Still, the thought of not poking into this made him uneasy. He wanted the truth to come out, and he didn't know if it would. He wasn't ready to dismiss this, no matter how much he should.

CHAPTER ELEVEN

"Relax. It's only Austin and Lacey," Eli said.

Dorran knew he was right. He forced his body to relax. It was just dinner, and it was with people Dorran was comfortable with. He should have been happy to be here, and he was. He also was uncomfortable with the fact that Lacey and Austin wanted to thank him with dinner, though. He didn't feel like he should be thanked for anything. He hadn't found the stalker. The stalker had revealed himself, and Dorran hadn't done anything.

Dorran still had doubts about Tony being the stalker, but he had stopped bringing them up, even with Eli. Even though Eli believed him and trusted Dorran's instincts, he wasn't in charge of the investigation. There was nothing he could do except tell Dorran to trust the police and his colleagues. After what had happened to his brother and his father, though, Dorran had little faith in them. He knew it wasn't fair, but he couldn't help it.

He didn't know Tony. They weren't friends, and they never would be. He shouldn't care if Tony paid for something he hadn't done, but he couldn't help it. He kept turning the case this way and that in his mind, trying to find the real stalker, wondering who it could be. He still had no idea, and he didn't think that would change anytime soon.

Maybe he really should let it go.

Eli knocked on the door of Lacey's apartment. He was more relaxed than Dorran, and Dorran plastered a smile on his face. Eli wanted him to be happy, and the only thing that was stopping him from that was his conviction that Tony wasn't the stalker. He wouldn't be able to do anything about it tonight, though. He might as well focus on dinner and his friends, and he could still come back to the case tomorrow or the day after that. Tony wasn't in jail, even though the police were looking into him. Nothing would happen to him even if he was accused, not for now.

The door opened. Austin smiled, but it was tense, and Dorran straightened his back, knowing something was wrong right away. He wasn't the only one.

Eli asked, "What's going on?"

Austin shook his head and leaned closer. "I'm sorry. This wasn't supposed to happen," he murmured.

Dorran frowned. "What wasn't supposed to happen?"

Austin waved them in and closed the front door behind them. "This dinner was to thank you, Dorran. It was supposed to be only the four of us, but one of Lacey's friends came by, and she invited herself for dinner." Austin grimaced. "I tried telling her to leave, but she just ignores what I'm saying."

That sounded rude, although Dorran understood why Austin hadn't insisted. He probably wouldn't have, either. He didn't have it in him.

"Don't worry about it," Eli said. "It's dinner. I don't see why she shouldn't stay."

Austin shook his head. "I wanted some family time with you two."

Dorran wasn't exactly happy about it, but this wasn't his apartment, and he wasn't the one making decisions. He'd been hoping to relax, but now, he doubted he would.

He should have known it was Heather, he told himself as soon as he stepped into the living room. She was standing there, drinking a glass of wine, looking put together perfectly. Her long hair hung over her shoulders, and she was smiling at Lacey. She turned when she heard them, and her expression hardened just for a second. Then, she smiled. "Dorran. I didn't know you were the one coming to dinner," she said.

Dorran had to bite his lower lip not to be rude. "It's a pleasure to see you again, Heather."

He suspected they both knew it was a lie. Heather's smile tightened. "Same."

Dorran moved closer to Eli. He didn't want anything to do with Heather. She'd made it very clear what she thought about him the first time they'd met, and he wasn't looking forward to being insulted again. "This is Elijah, my boyfriend."

Heather's smile seemed to be fixed on her face as she and Eli shook hands. "Austin's brother, right?" she asked.

"Right," Eli responded. "Now, if you'll excuse me, Austin said he needed me in the kitchen."

Dorran scowled at Eli, who blew him a kiss before disappearing and leaving Dorran in Heather's claws. Luckily for him, Heather seemed to be focused on Lacey tonight.

"You know, you should have listened to me when I told you that you shouldn't date Tony," she said.

Lacey was setting the table, and her cheeks flushed. "You already mentioned that, and I admitted you were right. How many times do I have to say it?"

"I'm sorry. I don't mean to be rude. I'm just saying that I saw through him right away, and I tried to warn you. You should have known better."

God. Dorran disliked Heather, and he wasn't sure why. He also wasn't sure why Lacey was friends with her. She was rude all the way around, starting with how she'd invited herself for dinner and continuing with the fact that she was telling Lacey that she'd been an idiot.

"I think she understands that she shouldn't have dated him," Dorran said.

Heather turned her attention to him and arched a brow. "Oh, really? You know, I told her that she should have gone to the police right away. I still don't understand why she came to you, to be honest. It's not like you did anything."

"I stopped Tony," Dorran said even though he knew he hadn't done anything like that.

Heather snorted. "You stopped him with your face? That bruise is impressive."

Dorran reached for his face before he could think better about it, and it took all he had not to scowl at Heather. "I did what I had to do."

"What you had to do was to find a stalker. You didn't. The stalker revealed himself."

Dorran shouldn't be rude to her, no matter how rude she was to him. He was a guest here, and even though Lacey looked uncomfortable, she wasn't saying anything about Heather's behavior.

"I mean, I could have told you it was him," Heather continued. "I told Lacey how stupid she was for being with him right from the beginning, but she didn't listen. She should have. See, Lacey? You should always listen to me. I'm smarter."

Dorran had enough. He looked around, trying to find Eli, who had disappeared sometime during the conversation, along with his brother. Since he could hear voices coming from the small kitchen, he headed toward it. He'd only been in the apartment once, when Tony had attacked Lacey, but he remembered where the kitchen was. He was relieved when he found Eli and Austin there, and he rushed toward his boyfriend.

Eli blinked at him and opened his arms, wrapping them around Dorran. "What's going on?"

Dorran shook his head. "Nothing."

Eli softly snorted and stroked Dorran's back. "We both

know that's a lie."

It was, but Dorran didn't want to tell Eli that he was running from Heather.

"You should ignore what she's saying," Austin said. "I don't like her, either, but she's Lacey's friend."

"Why?" Dorran asked before he could think better of it.

Austin laughed and shrugged. "I have no idea. I know Lacey and Heather met in college and that Heather was there when Lacey needed her. Her mom died, and she couldn't rely on her father. Heather has been hanging around since then."

Dorran could understand relying on a friend when you went through something like losing your mother, but *Heather*?

"Why don't we go home?" Eli asked.

"Already?" Austin answered. "You haven't even had dinner yet."

"I'm sorry. But it's obvious Dorran is uncomfortable with Heather here, and I don't want him to be. Maybe we can come back for dinner another time?"

"You're always welcome here, so yeah. I'm just sorry you're leaving me alone with her."

Dorran had never been so relieved that Eli could use his job as an excuse. He whisked them out of the apartment in only a few minutes, and Dorran didn't even have to see Heather again, since Lacey and Austin walked them to the door. He breathed more easily once they were outside, and he and Eli were silent as they headed back to the car.

"What's going on?" Eli asked.

Dorran shook his head. He felt ridiculous just thinking about it, and he didn't want to say it out loud. "Nothing."

"Come on. Tell me. I'm sorry I left you alone with Lacey and Heather. I shouldn't have."

"It's fine. I'm an adult. I can stand up to a woman."

"But something happened, didn't it?"

Dorran wasn't sure how to explain how he felt and what

he thought. "I don't like her."

Eli snorted. "From what Austin told me, I doubt anyone likes her."

He probably wasn't wrong about that. "It's more than that, though. You didn't hear how hard she was trying to make Lacey believe Tony is the stalker. And she was putting Lacey down, telling her how stupid she'd been, both for trusting Tony in the first place and for asking me to look into this. And that letter. I don't know if what Heather copied down for me was what was in that letter, but it felt so resentful." Dorran hesitated. He didn't understand why Heather would have written him the same letter she'd left for Lacey, but since she thought he was an idiot, maybe it made sense. "I think she might be the stalker," he said.

He expected Eli to tell him it was crazy, but to his surprise, Eli nodded. "You might be right."

"You think so?"

"It makes sense. She has an intimate relationship with Lacey, although not the kind we were thinking about. She probably also has the means to come and go in the apartment. You should ask Lacey, but I wouldn't be surprised if Heather had a key. She also knows a lot of personal details about Lacey, including where she works, her routine, and every-thing else."

"Why would she do this, though?"

"I don't know. I'm going to talk to the guys in charge of the investigation, but I don't know what will come out of it. We don't have proof of anything so far."

Dorran groaned. "Let me guess. You want me to look into it?"

Eli grimaced. "I think I do, yes. I know I told you that you shouldn't do this anymore only a few days ago, but if the stalker is still out there, and if it's Heather like you suspect, Lacey needs to know. She needs to be safe."

She did, but Dorran wasn't sure he could keep her safe.

CHAPTER TWELVE

Dorran was poking around social media again. Now that he had a new suspect, he couldn't wait to find something, *anything*, that would tell him that Heather was the stalker.

So far, it still was just an impression. He had no proof, and if he admitted it, no reason to suspect her. Yes, she was an asshole, and he didn't understand why Lacey was close to her, but that didn't make her a stalker.

He couldn't deny there were a lot of things pointing toward it, though. As he'd suspected, Heather had access to Lacey's apartment. He'd asked Lacey, and she'd confirmed that Heather came over to water the plants and grab the mail when Lacey traveled. That meant she would be able to sneak into the apartment any time, especially since she also knew Lacey's movements. She knew when Lacey was at work, and most of the time when Lacey stayed at Austin's apartment for the night. Dorran hadn't wanted to ask too many questions, but he was pretty sure Heather wouldn't have a problem entering the apartment and doing whatever she wanted, including stealing stuff from Lacey. She also knew where Lacey worked, so she could call Lacey's office, then hang up when she got Lacey on the phone. She would have known where Lacey was and slashed her tires as well.

It all fit. She knew a lot of intimate details about Lacey's life. She knew who everyone would suspect. Now that Dorran was examining everything and keeping Tony out of the equation, he could see that she was the perfect suspect, more so than Tony. What he didn't know was why she would do this.

He'd tried asking Lacey about her, hoping Lacey wouldn't realize there was something wrong with the questions. From what Lacey had explained, she and Heather had been friends for years, since college, like Austin had said. Heather had been there for Lacey when her mother had died, and she'd stuck around since then. The fact that Dorran found Heather unpleasant didn't mean she was a stalker, though. The statistics were clear. Men were more often stalkers than women, especially when the victim was a woman herself. That didn't mean it was impossible, but it did make things harder.

And it was the last thing Dorran needed.

He was relieved when his phone rang, and even more so when he saw Eli's name flash on the screen. He was ready for a break, so he answered right away. "Hey," he said. Eli didn't usually call him during the day, so there was always a hint of worry when he did, but Dorran forced himself to listen to what Eli had to say before panicking.

"Hey. Everything okay?" Eli asked.

"Yep. You?"

"Same." There was as rustling sound, then Eli said, "Listen, I have some news about Tony."

Dorran sucked in a breath. It could make or break his case.

And he really should stop thinking like a police officer.

"What is it?"

"Well, we worked with the assumption that the person who attacked Lacey the other night was her stalker."

That was one more thing that didn't fit. If Tony was the stalker and had been the one who'd attacked Lacey, then he would already know how she was. It didn't make sense for him to go find her the day after, although maybe he'd only done it to show that he cared about her and that he couldn't possibly hurt her.

Everything in this case was confusing.

"Did he admit to it? Was he the one who attacked Lacey?"

he asked.

"No. He had an alibi for the attack. He was at a bar with friends, and he was there for most of the night. He was there when Lacey was attacked. There's video evidence. He couldn't have been the one who attacked her."

"Anything else?" Dorran had suspected this would happen, and he was both relieved and dismayed about the fact that Tony had nothing to do with the stalking. He didn't like Tony much, but then he didn't know the man either. He only knew what Lacey had told him about him, and that was enough for him to form an opinion. Still, the fact that Tony was an asshole didn't mean he was a stalker.

"Apparently, he also doesn't have easy access to Lacey's apartment. He would have had to break in to steal her stuff, and she would probably have noticed, especially since it happened more than once. I think you're looking for someone who has a key, Dorran."

Heather and Austin were the only other ones who had a spare key as far as Dorran knew, and he was sure that Austin had nothing to do with this.

That left Heather.

Dorran wasn't quite sure what to do with this information, though. "Do you know if Lacey's father has a key?"

The hesitation on the other side of the line was enough to answer Dorran's question. "I have no idea. I can try asking, but again, this isn't my case. You'll probably have better results if you ask Lacey directly."

Dorran didn't want to do that. Lacey was convinced that Tony was her stalker and that she was safe now. Dorran doubted she would want to listen to him, especially if it was to tell her that Tony had nothing to do with it. Still, he was going to do it. Lacey needed to know she was still in danger, and it would be good if she also knew that Tony had nothing to do with the attack. He hadn't been the one to hurt her, not this time.

Dorran sighed. "I'll call her and ask." Because no matter how much Dorran disliked Heather, and how much things seemed to point at her, there was still the fact that it didn't make sense. She was Lacey's friend. She had been for years, while the stalker had only appeared a few months ago. If it was Heather, why had she waited? Why was she doing this now?

Dorran had no answers, but a lot of questions. He was starting to wonder if maybe he should ignore his instinct of suspecting Heather and focus on other people. He hadn't thought that Bill had anything to do with it, but he might be wrong. There was about the same chance that Heather was the stalker as Bill was.

"I have to go," Eli said. "Be careful . . . whatever you do. And if you leave the apartment, let me know. I want to know where you are, just in case. I should be home early tonight. We managed to wrap up the case we were focusing on, so we're taking off a few hours early."

After everything that had happened in the past, Dorran wasn't going to compromise on that. "I will. I'll text you if I leave."

"Be careful. Love you."

Dorran was still thinking about his problem when he and Eli hung up.

Heather was a good suspect, but Dorran had to admit Bill was, too. With Tony out of the picture, it seemed obvious that the stalker wasn't the usual one. Either it was Lacey's father, a man she did have a significant relationship with but who didn't fit the profile and was too blunt to be a stalker, or it was her best friend, a woman who didn't have a reason to stalk and hurt her. Dorran didn't want to focus on Heather and possibly be wrong and have Bill hurt Lacey.

He needed to go back to his list. He had to go over the

names again, especially now that he knew Tony was out. He had some strong suspicions that it was either Bill or Heather, but maybe he'd been wrong to strike out Sophie and Bridget.

He was right back at the beginning—lost and with no idea which way to go.

Dorran had to be crazy. It was the only explanation he had for the fact that he'd tracked down Bill to a bar near his house.

He wasn't even sure why. He was still hung up on Heather being the stalker, but he needed to be sure. At this point, either he was wrong and Bill was the stalker, Heather was, or it was someone Dorran and Lacey didn't know. Either way, Bill might be able to tell Dorran something about Heather. The situation seemed like a win-win as long as Bill didn't try to kill Dorran for asking too many questions and bugging him while he was at the bar.

Dorran didn't know how things would go, but he was about to find out. He'd texted Eli to tell him what was happening, and Eli hadn't been happy to find out what he was doing. Still, he hadn't tried to stop him. Dorran wasn't used to Eli being so lenient, but he supposed they were both learning how to be with each other. A few months ago, Eli would have ordered him to go home. Now, he'd just asked him to be careful and to make sure to stay in a public place.

That was more than fine with Dorran

He noticed Bill right away as he walked into the bar. It was still fairly early, only six in the afternoon, but Bill already had an empty beer glass in front of him as well as a fresh one. Dorran hesitated, then steeled himself and stepped closer. "Mr. Owen," he said.

Bill blinked at him. It took him a second to recognize Dorran, and when he did, he grimaced and groaned. "You again. What do you want?"

"Just to talk about Lacey."

"I have nothing to tell you. I told you that if she has a stalker, she needs to go to the police."

"They're involved now since Lacey was attacked."

That got Bill's attention. "She was?"

He might just be a good actor, but Dorran didn't think that was the case. As far as he was concerned, Bill wasn't a stalker. Still, he didn't want to relax, not yet, possibly not ever while he was with Bill. "Can I sit down?" he asked.

"If you have to."

Dorran sat. He didn't order anything because he wasn't planning on staying for long. "As I said, your daughter was attacked a few days ago."

"Is she okay?"

"She will be. She's shaken, but she's not physically hurt, just a few scratches."

"That's good. What do you want from me, though?"

"I just wanted to ask you if you remembered anything new?"

Bill crossed his arms over his chest and glared. "You still think it was me, don't you? You think I attacked her."

"Of course not."

"You do. That's why you're here. Did she send you, or are you doing this on your own? I have nothing to do with this. I might not have been a good father, but I would never attack her."

Bill's voice was rising, and Dorran got to his feet, just in case he had to make a swift escape. Someone moved into his vision, and he looked at the man who was now standing next to the table. To his surprise, it was Mel, Eli's partner.

"Is everything okay here?" he asked.

Dorran had no idea how to answer that. Luckily for him, Bill did. He pushed his chair away from the table and got to his feet. He swayed, a sign that the two beers on the table weren't his first, then shook his head. "Nothing is going on.

I'm going home, and you need to leave me alone." He glared at Dorran. "I have *nothing* to tell you. I didn't hurt Lacey. I'm not a good father, but I wouldn't hurt her. I don't want to see you again."

That was okay because Dorran wasn't planning on contacting him again.

He waited until Bill had left the bar to relax. When he did, he saw that Mel was looking at him, his head cocked. "Thank you," he said.

Mel shook his head. "That's fine. But you should go home, Dorran. This isn't a place for you."

Mel moved to leave, but Dorran caught his arm. Dorran snatched his hand back as soon as he touched Mel, but Mel stopped and looked at him. Dorran cleared his throat. "I'm sorry. I shouldn't have grabbed you."

"It's fine. Do you need anything?"

"Is Eli here?"

"No. He went home."

Because he'd told Dorran he would be home early. *Right.* "And you didn't?"

Mel looked around. "Home is empty right now. I thought I would grab a beer or something."

It was a bit early to do that, but Dorran didn't point that out. He knew Mel was having trouble with a lot of stuff, including coming to terms with the fact that he could see ghosts. "Do you want to have dinner with me?"

Mel blinked. "Dinner?"

"You know. It's that thing where you sit down and eat the stuff on your plate?"

Mel narrowed his eyes. "I didn't believe Eli when he said you were a smart mouth, but I see he was right." He sighed heavily. "You're not going to let this go, are you?"

"I think we need to talk."

"You're right." He looked around. "Come on. I know a

place."

Dorran was relieved they weren't going to have dinner at the bar. He followed Mel outside, already texting Eli to tell him he'd met his partner and that he wasn't coming home for dinner. Eli seemed to be okay with that. He even asked Dorran to make sure Mel was all right. He was aware of the fact that Mel was having trouble dealing with the ghost thing, and he probably wanted Dorran to help his partner come to terms with it.

Dorran wasn't sure he would be able to do anything, but he was going to try.

The place Mel selected was a small Italian restaurant. From the way the people around them reacted to his presence, it was obvious he came there often. They were taken to a small table in the back, and Mel sat in front of Dorran, staring at him. It made Dorran uncomfortable, but he didn't say anything about it.

"Ghosts," Mel eventually said.

Dorran's cheeks flushed. "Yeah. Pretty much."

Mel chuckled. "I would never have thought that was a thing. Although, now that I know about the entire situation, some of the things Eli said and *didn't* say make sense. How long have you been able to see them?"

Dorran tapped his fingertips on the table. "You remember that first case? When I met Eli for the second time?"

"The one where you found a body in the laundry room?"

"That one. He's not the ghost, though. The first ghost I was able to see was Francis. He was the former owner of the apartment, the one who was killed by his nephew."

Mel nodded. "I remember the case. He's still around?"

"He is. He shares the apartment with Eli and me."

"How do you deal with this?"

"Not well, at least not in the beginning. I won't deny it. It's not an easy thing to wrap your mind around. You can't avoid this for much longer, though."

"Why not?"

"Because for now, you've been doing a good job of ignoring the ghosts you see around. One day, though, some of them are going to realize that you can see them. Then they'll start bugging you. You and I are some of the few people who can talk to ghosts easily. Eli can see Francis, but that's because Francis is becoming stronger, and usually, I'm around when it happens. Some ghosts are weaker. Some are stronger. In some cases, though, you and I are the only people who can talk to them. They'll flock to you, demand that you contact their family or do something for them."

Mel groaned. "That sounds like hell."

"It can be. That's why you have to learn how to use your power. So you can shield yourself."

"I don't want to talk to ghosts."

"However you decide to use the gift, whether it's to talk to ghosts or to push them away, you need to know what's going on and how to use it. I can give you the number of the person who helped me, if you want. She can't work miracles, but she'll do everything she can for you."

Mel didn't look convinced, but when Dorran left the restaurant, he'd managed to push one of Carole's business cards to him. Hopefully, Mel would take it and call her. Dorran had no idea how hard this was for Mel, since they barely talked, but he could see the strain in the way Mel looked around continuously. He was searching for ghosts, and even though there hadn't been any in the restaurant tonight, Dorran suspected that Mel saw them more often than he'd admitted.

He wanted to help. He didn't know how, though. It was a step Mel needed to take, and the only thing Dorran could do was to be there for him.

Dorran needed to talk to Lacey again. He was getting

nowhere with what he had, and he couldn't stop thinking about his suspects. It was either Heather or Bill, and Dorran didn't know how Lacey would take that. She'd already shown that she wouldn't believe him if he told her he suspected her friend, so he wasn't sure how to bring it up. He felt he had to, though. If Heather was the stalker, Lacey needed to be aware of that.

Of course, there was no way to know whether she would listen to him.

He reached for his phone. It wasn't too late. Eli was waiting for him at home, and he wanted to go. He also wanted to warn Lacey, though. He wanted her to stay away both from Heather and Bill, just in case.

She answered after only a few rings. "Dorran. Is everything okay?"

Dorran couldn't help but smile at her worry. "I'm perfectly fine. How about you?"

She huffed. "Lonely. Austin had something to do with a friend tonight."

"Well, I'm not home yet. Do you want me to come over? I can stay with you for an hour or so until Austin comes back."

Dorran could hear a surprise in Lacey's voice when she answered. "You would do that?"

"Of course. Why shouldn't I?"

"I don't know. We're not exactly friends, are we?"

"Maybe not friends yet, no, but we're practically family."

"I guess that's true. I called Heather, but she's not answering her phone."

Dorran's heart skipped a beat. "Don't call her. I'll come by." He couldn't risk it. Even if Heather wasn't the stalker, he needed to be careful, and so did Lacey.

"Thank you," she said.

"I'll be right there. Don't worry."

Dorran took the time to text Eli to tell him what was going

on before he headed to Lacey's apartment. He didn't like the thought of her being alone, or worse, alone with Heather. He hoped she hadn't tried calling Heather again, but he couldn't be sure.

The whole situation freaked him out. He wanted to be good at this, to find out who the stalker was and why they were hurting Lacey, but he didn't know if he could. It wasn't his job, and he knew he shouldn't feel it as deeply as he was. Still, as far as he was concerned, he was responsible for Lacey's safety right now. She had asked him to look into this, and he'd agreed. That meant he should have answers for her.

But he didn't, not yet, and possibly not ever. Maybe he sucked at this. Maybe he was only good at solving murders. Hell, maybe he sucked at all of this, period, and the only reason he'd managed to find four murderers was that he'd had help from ghosts.

That was probably the case.

He wouldn't tell Lacey that, though. She trusted him with this, and he didn't want her to be afraid. Of course, he might already be too late for that. She had to be terrified after being attacked. He wanted to help her, but he didn't know if he could. There was one little thing he *could* do, though.

She was waiting for him when he got to her apartment. She smiled, standing at the open door, and ushered him inside. "Thank you for coming," she said.

"Don't worry about it. I wouldn't have suggested it if I didn't think it was a good idea."

"Still. I wish Heather would have answered her phone."

Dorran was relieved she hadn't. "Why don't we sit down?"

Lacey's eyes narrowed. "That sounds like you have to tell me something I won't like."

"Well, I doubt there's anything you *will* like in this situation."

"True. But you know something, don't you? You found

something, and you want me to sit down because you think I'm not going to like it."

Dorran forced himself to smile. "You caught me. Let's sit, okay?" He needed a few seconds to wrap his mind around what he needed to say and find a way to say it that wouldn't send Lacey into denial. He didn't know if that was possible, but he was going to try.

He cleared his throat once they were on the couch. "I talked to your father," he said.

"I know. You told me about it, remember?"

"I meant that I talked to him again after I found out that it couldn't have been Tony who attacked you the other night."

Lacey grimaced. "Austin told me about that."

"So you know it couldn't have been Tony. That means Tony probably isn't your stalker. I don't think your father is, either. If I have to be honest, he doesn't seem the type. He doesn't have a problem telling you what he thinks about you to your face, and he's not the subtle kind."

Lacey's shoulders slumped. "I think you're right. I'm kind of relieved, but also sorry. I don't want to think that my father would be able to do something like this, but he's also an asshole. Better him than someone I care about."

Dorran didn't blame her. "I think the stalker could be someone you don't know, but I doubt that's the case, too." He couldn't get the words out, but he knew he had to.

Lacey frowned. "How are we supposed to find out who it is, then?"

"I don't know how it would work in that case. But stalkers are usually someone who knows their victim intimately, so like I said, I don't think it's the case, either."

"You suspect someone."

Dorran nodded and opened his mouth to tell her about Heather, but someone knocked on the door, and Lacey's eyes widened. She looked at Dorran, probably expecting him to take charge.

He had no idea what to do. "I don't think the stalker would knock," he said.

By the time he realized how wrong he was, Lacey was already at the door. Of course the stalker would knock if it was Heather. She had a key, but she wouldn't just barge in, not when Lacey might be there.

Lacey opened the door, and Heather pushed past her to get in. "What's going on?" she asked. "I saw you called me."

Lacey frowned. "I did. You didn't answer."

Heather's gaze moved around the room and stopped when it got to Dorran. "So you called *him*? Seriously?"

Lacey looked confused. "I don't know what you're talking about. I didn't call Dorran. He called me, and when I told him that you weren't answering your phone, he suggested he could come by."

Heather's expression twisted. "Of course he did. Don't you see what he's doing? He's wiggling his way into your life."

"He doesn't have to. We're almost family. We're dating two brothers."

Heather's cheeks reddened. "You're not family. You're not married to Austin, and he's not married to his boyfriend."

"That doesn't mean we're not family. Besides, we're friends. That means more than family, doesn't it?"

"You're replacing me," Heather snapped.

Lacey took a step back. "What are you talking about? I'm not replacing you. How could I?"

Heather shook her head, stepping closer to Lacey. Lacey's back hit the wall, and Dorran held his breath. He had to do something, but what? He didn't want to make things worse by intervening.

"You're replacing me," Heather repeated. "After everything I did for you. After you cried on my shoulder when Tony cheated on you. After you didn't listen to me when I warned you. You're *replacing* me."

Lacey shook her head and reached for Heather, but Heather jerked back. "Please, Heather. You need to calm down," Lacey begged.

Heather reached into her purse, and Dorran sucked in a breath when she retrieved a gun from it. She pointed it at Lacey, who looked like she might faint. "I don't need to do anything. *You* need to sit down and shut up."

CHAPTER THIRTEEN

Dorran held his breath. He could tell saying the wrong thing would make Heather snap, and that was obviously the last thing he and Lacey needed. They had to keep Heather calm while someone came to help them.

Dorran had no idea if someone would, though. No one knew what was happening. That meant he was going to have to do something to save himself and Lacey.

His phone was in his pocket. Heather was focused on Lacey, and Dorran hoped he could slip it out and speed-dial Eli—and keep Heather from noticing. It was the only hope they had, and he couldn't waste it.

He made sure to move as little as he could. He breathed more easily when the phone was out of his pocket, but he still wasn't done. Luckily for him, Eli was number one on speed-dial, and Heather was still ranting at Lacey, who was pressed against the wall, her eyes so wide they might pop out of their sockets.

He unlocked his phone, called Eli, then hid the phone under the pillows on the couch. He hoped Eli would be able to hear what was going on even through the fabric, but he couldn't be sure. He also couldn't make sure whether Eli answered. Heather might notice.

Then Dorran raised his hands to his chest to make sure Heather knew he wasn't a danger. Now that he'd done everything he could, he wanted to distract Heather and turn her attention to him rather than Lacey. If someone was going to get hurt, he would rather have it be him than her.

"You don't need a gun," he told Heather. He swallowed when the gun turned toward him. He'd wanted this, but now he was getting nervous.

"Shut up."

Dorran raised his hands higher. "I'm not trying to do anything. I'm just not comfortable with a gun pointed at my face."

"You'd be even less comfortable if I shot you."

That much was true.

Dorran swallowed again. His mouth was dry, but he needed to speak through it. He needed to speak through the fear that gripped his gut and made him think he couldn't get to his feet even if he tried. "Me being Lacey's friend doesn't mean that you're not her friend anymore," he said slowly. "Besides, the only reason Lacey and I have been spending time together is because of the stalker. Because of *you*."

Lacey paled and shook her head, but Dorran kept his attention on Heather. He was pretty sure telling her to her face he knew she was the stalker would make things worse, but it might not, and he needed to do *something*.

He cleared his throat. "I can't do anything about Lacey being family, but let's be honest. We're not actually friends. We never talked before I met her at Sunday lunch, and even though she's a nice woman, I don't think we mesh well. She needs me. That's why we've been spending time together. You're doing a much better job at being her friend than I can, though."

Heather's hand tightened around her gun. "Shut up," she snapped. "I don't want you to open your mouth. This is between Lacey and me. You have nothing to do with this. Everything was perfect before you stuck your nose into it, and I should shoot you and be done with you. That would teach you."

Dorran prayed he wasn't going to leave the apartment with a few more holes in him than he'd had when he walked in. "I understand."

Heather laughed darkly. "I don't think you do. No one understands." She turned the gun back toward Lacey. "I should be you."

Dorran had no idea what that meant. He wasn't about to ask, either.

"I don't understand," Lacey said softly. She didn't seem to be as afraid as Dorran was, which didn't make sense. Maybe she was just better at hiding it.

Heather waved the gun around. "You have a perfect life. It's not fair. I *deserve* your life. I met Austin before you did, and he's the perfect boyfriend. He should be mine, not yours. And your job, your apartment, all of that. What do you have that I don't? Nothing."

"I don't—"

Dorran was starting to understand. Heather was jealous. She wanted to take Lacey's place, and apparently, she thought that stalking Lacey was a good way to make that happen. She'd terrified a woman who was supposed to be her friend, and she didn't seem to regret it.

Heather thrust the gun toward Lacey. "I deserve everything you have, and I'm going to take it. I was going to do things the right way, but this guy had to stick his nose into it, and that, too, is entirely your fault."

Dorran cleared his throat, trying to get Heather's attention back. "She didn't know what she was doing. She didn't know what was happening."

"I told you to shut up!"

Dorran was pretty sure his hands were going to get stuck raised the way they were if he stayed like this for much longer. He eyed the pillows, praying the phone call had gone through and that Eli had answered. Eli was their only hope, and while Dorran didn't like it, he didn't exactly have any better idea—or any other idea, period.

"I'm sure Lacey will be more than happy to give you anything you want," he murmured.

Heather shook her head. "She won't have to give them to me. I'm going to take *everything*."

That was exactly what Dorran was afraid of. "You were planning to kill her all along, weren't you?"

Heather licked her lips. "I never wanted to hurt her. I just wanted what was mine. I still do, and now, it's finally going to be."

This was terrifying. Dorran had been in this kind of situation before, but knowing Heather didn't have a good reason to be doing this was scarier. Some of the murderers he'd faced had had a normal reason to kill. They hadn't been unhinged. For some, it had been an accident. Others had killed because they'd been pushed to it. Heather, on the other hand, wasn't thinking clearly, and Dorran suspected she hadn't been for a long time. That meant she would shoot without thinking twice, which was what they needed to avoid.

Heather paced the length of the living room. "I wanted things to be easy for you. I was going to poison you so you wouldn't feel pain. But now you ruined everything, and you deserve to feel it. You deserve to die." Heather smiled. "But don't worry. I'll take good care of your apartment and your boyfriend. I'll be there to comfort him after you die, and I'll make sure he knows how much I loved you. It will be natural when we finally get together, but I'll make sure he remembers you." She paused and frowned. "But not too much."

Dorran didn't know what to do. He suspected Heather was about to shoot, but he was too far away to do anything. He couldn't stop her, and he couldn't put himself between the gun and Lacey. He needed a distraction, something that would give him a few seconds, enough to grab Lacey and get her out of the apartment.

That was when Francis appeared. He did so in front of the

door, away from Lacey and Dorran, but still in Heather's sight. She jerked, turning the gun toward him.

Dorran had no idea what he was doing, but he did know that this was his only chance to act. He pushed himself off the couch and threw himself at Heather, pushing her back.

A shot rang loud in the room.

Dorran didn't have the time to stop and make sure he was okay. He needed to get Lacey to safety.

He pushed Heather toward the wall, and she stumbled. The gun went wide, but it only took her a few seconds to gather herself. Dorran took advantage of those few seconds, grabbing Lacey's arm and pushing her deeper into the apartment. "Let's go," he yelled.

Thankfully, he didn't have to repeat himself. Lacey might be terrified, but she wasn't frozen in place. She took Dorran's hand and pulled him toward the bedroom. They staggered into it, Dorran only stopping to slam the door behind them. They looked at each other, their eyes wide, panting.

"Why did you do that?" Lacey asked.

Dorran had no answer to give her since she hadn't seen Francis. He turned to the door, relieved to see it could lock. He flipped the lock, then looked around. "Help me push the dresser in front of the door."

He hadn't thought it possible, but Lacey's eyes went even wider. "You think she's going to try to kick down the door?"

"I wouldn't put it past her. Better safe than sorry."

Lacey nodded curtly, then went to the dresser and grabbed everything that was on it. She threw it onto the bed, then started pushing the dresser toward Dorran. Dorran took the other side of it and pulled, and together, they managed to get it in front of the door.

Not one second too soon. Heather was already there, hitting the door, screaming at them from the other side. "I'm going to get to you! And when I do, you'll regret all of this. You hear me, Lacey? You should have kept only me as your friend. You shouldn't have betrayed me. You shouldn't have taken my life. You're going to pay for that."

Lacey shook her head. "I don't understand."

Dorran didn't either, and honestly, he didn't care. It didn't matter to him why Heather was behaving this way. It didn't matter if she had some psychiatric problems or if she was just a murderous bitch. He just wanted her to *stop.*

"Do you have your phone with you?" He'd left his on the couch. He hoped Heather wouldn't find it, but he couldn't be sure the call had connected with Eli. What if Eli hadn't answered? What if he had no idea what was happening? He wasn't expecting Dorran for a few hours yet, and Dorran didn't know what he would do if he and Lacey had to be stuck here for much longer. Heather was pissed, and eventually, she might find a way in.

To his dismay, Lacey shook her head. "It's in the kitchen. I left it there."

Dorran briefly closed his eyes. "Okay. That's a no-go." He moved to the window, looking out. "And we can't leave from here, either."

Lacey's eyes filled with tears. "I'm so sorry."

"Don't be. You have nothing to do with this."

"I involved you. Heather is my best friend. I should have known."

Dorran couldn't deal with Lacey if she broke down. He grabbed her shoulders and forced her to look at him. "You didn't know. Heather might be nuts or whatever she is, but she's also good at hiding it. She's a stalker. She knew exactly how to sneak into your apartment to steal your things. She knew when you went to work and when you would be home. She knew when you spent the night at Austin's. You trusted her. You *couldn't* have known."

Lacey nodded, then jumped when something heavy hit the door. "What is she doing?" she murmured.

Dorran shook his head. He had no idea, and he wasn't looking forward to finding out. "We have to find a way to let someone know we're in trouble."

"You don't have your phone with you?" Lacey asked.

"I got it out when Heather came in with a gun. I speed-dialed Eli, but I couldn't tell if he answered. I left the phone hidden on the couch."

Lacey bit her lower lip. "I don't know. What are we going to do?"

At this point, Dorran hoped a neighbor would realize what was happening. At the very least, someone had to hear the noise Heather was making. Of course, that might also be a bad thing. What if someone came in, wondering what was going on, and Heather shot them? So far, she'd only been violent toward Lacey and Dorran, but there was no way to know that would continue. She was unhinged, angry, and Dorran didn't know how she would react to someone interrupting her.

Heather pounded on the door again. "I'm going to kill you, Lacey! I'm going to kill you, then I'm going to take your life. I'm going to become you."

A door slammed, and Dorran held his breath. Heather screeched, and another shot echoed through the apartment. It was muted this time, on the other side of the door, but it still made Dorran jump. Who was Heather shooting at? Was it a neighbor?

Dorran moved closer to the door, making sure to stay on the side of it just in case Heather shot through it, and listened. Lacey came behind him, wrapping her arms around his waist and pushing close. He wasn't usually one for hugging, especially not with people he barely knew, but he patted her hand instead of asking her to move away. If he was honest, he could use the comfort, too.

"Put your weapon down!" a man yelled.

Dorran held his breath. Was it Eli? It sounded like it. And even if it wasn't, whoever the man was, he sounded like he knew what he was doing. That was a relief.

"You can't do this!" Heather yelled. "I haven't done anything. They're inside my apartment. They broke in and locked themselves in the bedroom. I'm just defending myself."

Dorran sucked in a breath. If whoever was talking to Heather believed her, if it was a police officer, he and Lacey might be in trouble. Lacey could no doubt prove that she rented this apartment, but that would mean they'd have to leave the room, and it would put them in danger.

"Put the weapon down," another man said. "I know this is Lacey's apartment, Heather. We were both here for dinner a few days ago, remember?"

Dorran slumped with relief. That *was* Eli. That meant that the other man was probably Mel and that Dorran and Lacey were safe. He turned around and dragged her into his arms. "We'll be fine. Eli is here."

She looked up, her eyes and cheeks wet. "Are you sure?"

"I recognize his voice. We'll be okay. They're going to take care of Heather, and we'll be safe." Dorran wasn't looking forward to having to stay in the bedroom for much longer, but he didn't want to risk it. He and Lacey stayed there, leaning against the wall. He made sure to be the one closest to the door, just in case he needed to protect her. The screams and protests on the other side of the door faded eventually, and Dorran and Lacey jumped when someone knocked on the door.

"Dorran?"

Dorran let go of Lacey. "We need to move the dresser. It's Eli."

"Are you sure? What if Heather is still there?"

Dorran shook his head. "He wouldn't knock if she were."

Still, Dorran should make sure so Lacey would be more comfortable leaving the bedroom. He called out, "Eli?"

The relief was evident in Eli's voice when he answered. "Dorran? You're in there?"

"We are. Can we come out? Is Heather still there?"

"We took care of her. We arrested her, and Mel walked her to the door. You don't have to worry about her anymore. She's handcuffed, and she can't hurt you and Lacey."

Dorran looked at Lacey again and gave her the time to think things out. He wanted to rush out and throw himself into Eli's arms, but he couldn't, not until Lacey agreed to it.

She finally nodded.

"We'll come out," Dorran said. "Give us a moment. We need to move the dresser we dragged behind the door."

"I'm not going anywhere," Eli answered. "I'll be right here when you open the door."

Dorran had never been so relieved and happy.

Dorran flung the door open as soon as the dresser had moved enough to allow it. Eli stood there, waiting, and he'd never looked so good. He didn't say anything, just opened his arms, and Dorran threw himself into them. They wrapped around him, holding him close, and he managed to hold back the sob that rose from his throat as he buried his face against Eli's neck.

"Are you okay?" Eli asked.

Dorran nodded. "I'll be fine. She didn't hurt us." They'd been lucky. When he'd heard that shot, he'd been convinced he'd been hit. He hadn't stopped to think about it, but he realized now that he hadn't been. He would be in pain and bleeding if that were the case.

"Can you tell me what happened?" Eli asked.

That would mean Dorran had to move away from him, but then, he probably should. Lacey was still in the bedroom, and no doubt, she was terrified. Eli had to do his job, and Dorran should make sure Lacey was okay.

He nodded again, then took a step back. He sucked in a breath, and even though it was hard to breathe, it was easier than before. He looked around. The apartment was crawling with cops. Eli had called the cavalry, and they'd arrived in time to save Dorran and Lacey. Dorran didn't think he'd ever been so grateful to see cops.

Eli gently touched his arm. "Why don't the two of you come to the living room? We can sit on the couch and talk about what happened."

Dorran nodded and reached back. Lacey took his hand, and together, they walked to the couch. They hadn't been friends before this, but he suspected they would be from now on. Facing death the way they had had pushed them together, and Dorran knew they would always share their experience.

They settled onto the couch, and Dorran let go of Lacey's hand to grab his phone. Eli had answered, but by now, he'd hung up, and the screen was dark. He put it into his pocket, then turned his attention to Eli. Mel stood behind the couch, talking on his phone, while Heather was nowhere to be seen.

For once, Dorran had managed to close the case with no one dying.

"What happened?" Eli asked.

"I called Lacey. I wanted to talk to her about her father."

"I told Dorran I was alone. Austin is with a friend." Lacey sucked in a breath. "I need to call Austin."

"You'll be able to call him as soon as we're done here. Why don't you text him to say that everything is okay? That way, if he comes here and sees the cops, he won't freak out."

Lacey stood up. "My phone is in the kitchen."

"We'll be here."

While she was gone, Dorran continued, "I decided to come over. I was scared for Lacey." He wanted to get this over with as soon as possible.

"Because you suspected Heather was the stalker," Eli said.

Mel had hung up and moved closer. He was listening to the conversation, but he didn't ask anything, so Dorran continued. The last thing he wanted was to go over what had happened again, but it was necessary. "She made sense," he explained. "She has a key, and she knows Lacey's timetable. She would be able to come in when Lacey wasn't home and take her things, as well as leaving the letter where she knew Lacey would find it."

"She has a key and knows all of that because she's Lacey's best friend," Mel pointed out. "It doesn't mean she's the stalker."

Dorran glared at him. "I wasn't sure she was the stalker, of course. I'm not a cop. It's not my job to be sure of those things. But I suspected her, and I didn't want to risk it. I decided to come over until Austin came home. Lacey was alone when I arrived, but Heather came soon after. Lacey opened the door, and it was obvious that Heather was upset. She was ranting, telling Lacey that she'd been there for her, that Lacey was replacing her with me, stuff like that. She was out of control." Dorran could too easily remember all of that, and he would have nightmares. He supposed he was used to it by now, anyway. This would be yet another nightmare to add to the long list of the ones he had at least once a week.

"Did she have the gun in hand when she came in?" Eli asked, his voice gentle.

Dorran shook his head. "She had a purse. Lacey let her in and closed the door. Heather was yelling. Then she took the gun out of her purse. She threatened both of us with it. She said she was going to kill Lacey and take her life, that she deserved Austin, the apartment, and Lacey's job more than Lacey did. She insulted Lacey, told her she was stupid for trusting Tony and for not listening to her. She didn't make a lot of sense." Yet in some ways, she had. She'd been right about Tony, and she'd no doubt made sure Dorran and Lacey suspected him. The only reason Tony had saved himself was that he'd had an alibi for the night of the attack.

Lacey stepped back into the living room and made a bee-line for the couch. She was clinging to her phone, and she nodded at Eli. "He's coming. I texted him, and he called me right away, so I answered."

Luckily, Eli didn't seem to be angry. "That's fine. Can you tell me what happened after Heather got the gun out?" he asked.

Dorran could answer, and he knew both he and Lacey would have to be interrogated separately, so he let her take over.

Lacey frowned. "She started yelling at me. I don't know why she felt that way about all of this. I never wanted to replace her."

"I doubt that anything makes sense in this situation. We're going to have a doctor see her, of course."

"A psychiatrist?"

"Yes. There's nothing written in stone right now, though. And I do need to hear what happened next."

Lacey slowly nodded. "She threatened both of us with a gun. I didn't know that Dorran had managed to call you, but I'm grateful. When Heather turned her attention to me after yelling at Dorran, I thought she was going to shoot me. I think that's what she was planning to do, but something distracted her, and Dorran jumped her."

Eli's eyes widened, and he looked at Dorran. Dorran suspected he would be yelled at eventually, but he shrugged. "What distracted her?" Eli asked.

Dorran bit his lower lip. He couldn't tell Lacey about ghosts and Francis. He wasn't even sure Heather had seen him. "I have no idea. I just know that she looked away for a moment, and I took the chance. I jumped on her and pushed her. She stumbled, and that's when I grabbed Lacey and we ran to the bedroom. I have no idea what happened next. We locked the door and waited for help to arrive."

"She shot Dorran," Lacey said. "I'm sure of that. I heard it."

Eli reached for Dorran, but Dorran shook his head. "She didn't hit me. I'm pretty sure the bullet hit the wall or something. I promise. I'm fine."

Eli was obviously torn between his role as a boyfriend and a detective, and Dorran, more than anyone, wished he could crawl into his boyfriend's lap and stay there for the rest of the night. Instead, he swallowed. "I'm not sure what distracted her," he said slowly, hoping Eli would understand what he was doing.

Eli's eyes widened slightly, and he nodded. "I see. So she got distracted, and you took that chance."

Dorran nodded. As he did so, a movement caught the corner of his eye. He didn't turn to look at whatever it was, but he smiled when he realized it was Francis. He was still around, making sure Dorran was okay. Dorran owed him his life. He didn't know if he would ever be able to thank Francis enough, but he would definitely try.

There was a commotion at the door, and someone yelled. Eli jumped to his feet and headed there, only to come back with Austin, who rushed to Lacey's side and pulled her into his arms. "Oh, my God. What happened? I can't believe she did this. Are you okay?"

Dorran got up and stepped away. Lacey was physically okay, but it would take her some time to wrap her mind around what had happened. They'd shared this traumatic experience, but Dorran knew what was next. He'd been through it already, so it was nothing new.

"Was it a ghost?" Eli asked quietly.

"Francis. I don't know how he knew he had to follow me,

but he did. He's still around." And Dorran suspected that was why Mel looked uncomfortable.

"We'll talk at home, okay?"

Dorran nodded again. "When will you be back?"

"We'll drive you home. Then we can talk about what actually happened."

That was more than okay with Dorran. He couldn't wait to leave this place. He'd liked Lacey's apartment before, but he doubted he would ever be able to spend any amount of time here anymore. He *definitely* wasn't about to come over for dinner.

CHAPTER FOURTEEN

"Okay," Eli said as soon as they were home. "What *actually* happened?"

Dorran sighed. He, Eli, and Mel had left Lacey's apartment a while ago. She'd been in good hands, and there had been nothing else Eli and Mel could do for her. Heather had been arrested, and she wouldn't be getting out tonight. Dorran didn't know what would happen tomorrow, but he could think about that later. Right now, the only thing he wanted to focus on was that he was home, that he was safe, and that he was never leaving his apartment again.

"It was Francis. He distracted her." He turned to look at Mel, wondering how he would take Francis' apparition. He didn't know, but he supposed he was about to find out. "Francis? Are you around?"

Of course, Francis was. He appeared in the middle of the living room, and Mel made a strangled sound and took a step back. Dorran ignored him, striding toward his friend. He wanted to hug Francis, but he couldn't, so he just reached for him, stopping before his fingers could touch him. "I would probably be dead if you hadn't been there," he murmured.

Francis shrugged. "I didn't do anything. I just appeared."

"You distracted Heather long enough for Lacey and me to get to safety. Thank you. You saved my life. *Our* lives."

Dorran was pretty sure Francis would have blushed if he could have. Instead, he shuffled awkwardly and looked away. "I was worried about you. You were taking this to heart, and I was afraid the stalker would get to you. I decided to follow you."

"How did you do that?"

"I clung to your phone. You take it everywhere."

Dorran barked out a laugh. "I do."

Eli cleared his throat. "So you decided to step in when Heather threatened Dorran?" he asked.

"Pretty much. I knew something was going to happen to Dorran. It does every time he sticks his nose into an investigation. He always gets hurt and shot at, and I wanted to avoid that. So when I realized that woman was going to shoot, I appeared. I was hoping it would help, and I was right. I was terrified for a second when that woman shot, but I don't think Dorran was hit." Francis scrunched his nose. "You weren't, right? I know you said you were fine to Eli, but you're home now. You can be honest."

"I'm fine," Dorran confirmed. "She didn't hurt me."

Dorran looked at Mel and realized Mel was freaking out. Now that Dorran thought about it, he doubted Mel knew who Francis was. He'd explained, and Mel might be able to recognize him, but seeing Francis was something else. "This is Francis," he explained. "He's the man who lived here before I moved in."

Mel nodded curtly. "I know."

"He won't hurt you," Dorran said. "He's friendly, and even Eli has gotten used to having him around."

Mel blinked and looked at Eli. "You're taking this well," he said.

Eli shrugged. "Yeah."

"You can see ghosts, too?"

Eli shook his head. "Only Francis, and only when he wants me to. Right?" he asked Dorran.

"Right," Dorran confirmed. "Francis is getting stronger because he's been dead for a while, and because he lives with me."

"What does that mean?" Mel asked.

"Ghosts can take strength from the people who can see them. Psychics. And that's what we are, whether or not you like it. We see ghosts even when they just died, and they can draw energy from us to be visible to other people, too. That's what Francis has been doing. Although now, he's strong enough on his own to be able to do it without me there."

Mel shook his head and rubbed his face. "I don't want to know any of this."

"I think you and Eli should talk," Dorran said. He wanted to go to bed, and he knew Eli had to go to the station. He might have already been home when Dorran had called him, but he'd taken things in hand, and he probably needed to write a report or something like that.

Dorran wasn't looking forward to being alone in the apartment, but he also wanted to shower. He felt dirty, as if Heather had soiled him. He needed to relax, maybe to cry for a bit. He wouldn't be able to do that when Eli was there. He didn't want his boyfriend to worry even more than he already was, and that was what would happen if he did.

"What am I supposed to tell him?" Eli asked.

"You didn't believe in ghosts when we met. Then, even after you saw ghosts and you realized that I really could talk to them, you did your best to deny and ignore it. Now you've accepted it, and you talk to Francis regularly. Talk to Mel, explain to him what happened and how you managed to wrap your mind around it and accept it." Dorran turned his attention to Mel. "And you. Call Carole. You need to learn to push ghosts away. Otherwise, you'll have to deal with them even when you don't want to."

Mel shook his head, and Dorran expected him to tell him he wasn't ready or something like that. Instead, Mel said, "I don't want to call your friend. I want *you* to help me."

Dorran took a step back. "I'm not a teacher."

"But you do this, don't you? You can push ghosts away."

"Because Carole taught me."

"Then you can teach me, too. Please. I already know you, and I trust you. No offense to your friend, but I don't know if I could trust her. Not with this."

Dorran could see it wasn't something Mel would compromise on. Either Dorran helped him, or he wouldn't do this, and eventually, his life would be overrun with ghosts. Dorran didn't have a choice. "I can try," he said. "But I'm not making any promises. I've never had to teach this. I barely learned myself."

"That's good enough for me." Mel cleared his throat, clearly done with the discussion. "We should get to the station," he told Eli.

Eli looked at Dorran, and Dorran knew what he was thinking. He forced himself to smile, even though he didn't feel like it. "Go. I already knew you'd have to, and I'm fine. I'm going to shower and get into bed."

"Are you sure? Because I can stay. Mel can do this on his own. Actually, it's probably better if he does."

"The captain is going to want to talk to us and to know why we intervened. We won't be in charge of this, but we need to explain what happened, and the sooner we do that, the better it will be."

"Fine. But we should also talk to the people in charge of the investigation. I want to know what's happening."

"And we will—both of us. The sooner you get this over with, the better it will be for Dorran. Come on. Let's head out."

Dorran had to reassure Eli he was okay a few more times before Eli finally agreed to leave. As soon as the door was closed behind them, Dorran turned to look at Francis, who was still standing in the middle of the living room.

Francis looked around. "I guess you want some peace?"

Dorran laughed. "Eventually, yes. You can stay here, though. I just don't want you to follow me into the bathroom." He swallowed. "Thank you. I don't know what I would have done if you hadn't been there to help."

Francis snorted. "I know exactly what you would have done, and what would have happened. I wouldn't mind having the company of the ghostly kind, but I'd rather you live a long and happy life."

Dorran hadn't expected that. "You'd want to spend the afterlife with me?"

Francis smiled. "I love you, Dorran." His eyes widened. "Like a nephew, or maybe a grandkid. Family, not anything else."

Dorran shook his head, but he was smiling. "Same. I love you too, Francis."

"Good. I want you to live. You need to be more careful. You're going to end up dead eventually, and while there's space here for both of us to haunt the apartment, I don't want that to happen."

"I'm never sticking my nose into this kind of situation again."

Francis rolled his eyes. "We both know that's not going to happen. But I'll be there if you need me."

Dorran knew he was lucky. No matter what happened, he would always have Francis and Eli. He wasn't kidding, though. He was never getting involved in any kind of crime ever again. It wasn't good for his health.

CHAPTER FIFTEEN

Dorran was once again not looking forward to Sunday lunch, although it was for different reasons this time. He already knew Eli's mother would fuss over him. She knew what had happened. The entire family did, and Dorran wasn't looking forward to facing them. They would be all over him, even though he hadn't done anything. At least he'd be able to make sure Lacey was okay with his own two eyes.

She'd called him after what had happened with Heather. She'd thanked him, sobbing, and Dorran hadn't been sure what to say to make her feel better. He doubted anything would after what had happened with Heather.

There wasn't a valid reason for what Heather had done. She was being evaluated by several psychiatrists, and as far as Dorran was concerned, it wouldn't be a bad thing if she stayed wherever she was for the rest of her life. But if she was sick, if that was the reason that she'd hurt Lacey, then she needed to have help.

Dorran should probably care more, but she'd shot at him. Even though she hadn't hit him, she'd still been trying to kill him, and he couldn't forgive that, no matter how unwell she was. Whatever happened, she would never be part of Lacey's life again. Lacey had been clear, and she didn't even want to talk to her former best friend. Dorran didn't blame her.

"Ready?" Eli asked from the driver seat.

Dorran shook his head. "Why can't we go home?"

"I'm pretty sure Mom would come and drag you back. You know she wants to see you."

"Because she wants to fuss. Did you tell her I'm okay?"

"Of course I did. It's not going to stop her, though."

Dorran knew it, which was why he didn't want to go in. Still, there was no way out of it, and after sighing heavily, he opened the passenger door and stepped out.

The front door opened as soon as he closed the car door. Eli's mother stood there, drying her hands on a towel. "I was starting to think the two of you would never come in," she said.

Dorran suck in a breath, plastered a smile on his face, and went to her. "We were just talking."

She opened her arms and dragged Dorran into them. "Are you sure? Are you feeling unwell?"

"I'm fine."

"Austin told me what happened. What you did."

Dorran grimaced before stepping away from the embrace. "I didn't *do* anything."

"You saved Lacey's life." She ushered Eli and Dorran in and closed the door. "That means the world to us."

"Anyone would have done it."

"Maybe so, but you were the one who actually did it, weren't you? Come on. Everyone wants to see you."

The half-hour before lunch was a whirlwind of people talking to Dorran, asking him how he was, thanking him for what he'd done, and patting his shoulders and arms. He limited himself to smiling and answering the questions thrown at him, but by the time lunch was on the table, he was grateful to be able to escape to the bathroom for a moment to wash his hands.

He leaned against the sink and took a deep breath. He should be grateful for this. Eli's family had accepted him, and this was another sign of that. They were happy to see he was okay, and that meant he was part of the family. It was what he'd wanted since the beginning, so why was he feeling like this?

He knew why. He wanted to forget all about Heather. He wanted to forget what had happened in Lacey's apartment, yet when people asked him about it, he couldn't. There was no way out of it. He was sure that sooner or later, something else would happen, and everyone would get distracted. In the meantime, though, he would have to deal with it.

So that was what he did. He left the bathroom and almost collided with Austin. Austin grabbed him before Dorran could fall on his ass and smiled at him. "I'm glad I got you alone."

Dorran looked around. "That doesn't sound good."

Austin laughed. "It's nothing. I just wanted to thank you for what you did for Lacey." He swallowed heavily. "If you hadn't come to her apartment when she needed you. If you hadn't been there . . ."

Dorran knew what would have happened. They both did. "But I did, and I helped her. You need to stop thinking about it. It's no use obsessing over the fact that you weren't there or what could have happened. It *didn't* happen."

Austin nodded and rubbed his face. "She's feeling bad, you know? She trusted Heather. They were best friends. She feels betrayed in the worst way. Heather was the only person Lacey confided in most of the time, and now, her trust has been broken."

"Do you know why Heather did this? Apart from the jealousy, I mean." Dorran had promised himself he didn't care, but he was curious. There had to be something else. People were jealous all the time, yet they didn't stalk their best friends.

"I'm not sure. I don't care, but Lacey does. The doctors think there's something wrong with Heather. I don't know what, and I'm not going to ask. But if it helps give Lacey peace of mind, then I don't mind if she looks into it. As long as

Heather is out of our lives, I'm fine with anything."

"I understand."

"Lacey feels guilty that she never suspected Heather. We were lucky that no one was seriously hurt, but Lacey was terrified for so long."

Dorran was grateful when he and Austin finally got to the dining room. He didn't want to talk about this again, or even to think about it. He was over it. It had been his last case as a wannabe detective, and it was over. He was more than grateful to go back to his translations, even though it could be boring some days.

Everything went back to normal during lunch. People talked and laughed around Dorran, and he relaxed. Whatever happened, this was his family. He knew it deep in his chest, and he couldn't help the stupid smile on his lips.

The smile grew even larger when Austin got to his feet, getting everyone's attention. He took Lacey's hand, and they looked at each other. It was enough for Dorran to know what he was about to say. This kind of mystery, he didn't mind investigating.

"I asked Lacey to marry me," Austin announced.

His mother made a strangled sound, and her hands flew to her lips.

"And what did she say?" Julian asked. He paused. "Wait. Don't tell me. She said no. Who would want to marry your ass?"

"Well, *you* found someone who wanted to marry you, and you're worse than me."

Everyone laughed, and Lacey shook her head. "I said yes. Of course."

The next ten minutes were busy with congratulations, hugs, and kisses. Dorran squeezed Lacey in a hard hug when it was his turn, murmuring, "Congratulations. I know the two of you will be happy."

There were tears in Lacey's eyes when she leaned back. "We already are. But what happened made us see we shouldn't wait. There's no reason to. We love each other. We both want this, and when I think about what we could have lost . . ."

"But you didn't lose Austin, and now you're getting married."

Lacey nodded. "We are."

Dorran went back to his seat. He couldn't stop smiling, and that was a huge difference from when he'd arrived earlier. He grinned at Eli, feeling better, and stuffed a meatball into his mouth.

Eli's mother looked at him, then at Eli. "So, Eli. When are you going to make an honest man out of Dorran?"

Dorran almost suffocated himself with the meatball. He grabbed his glass of water, sucking it down as he tried to breathe. His heart was racing, and he was afraid to look at Eli. His boyfriend never did well when he was pushed.

But for some reason, Eli didn't look like he was about to run away when Dorran finally peeked his way. He was clearly embarrassed, but he stroked Dorran's back until Dorran managed to breathe again.

Dorran hadn't expected this. Eli's mother might have accepted their relationship, and she might even like Dorran now, but that was a long way from wanting to see Eli and Dorran get married. She was smiling, everyone was listening, and Dorran didn't know how to react.

He turned his attention to Eli. "Yes, Eli. When are you going to make an honest man out of me?" Better throw Eli the ball so Dorran wouldn't have to come up with an answer.

Eli's cheeks flushed. "Shut up. We just moved in together."

"Lacey and I never moved in together," Austin pointed out. "Doesn't mean I'm not going to marry her."

Eli threw a piece of bread at his brother's face. "When the

moment comes, I'll know. We're in no rush."

That was enough for Dorran. He leaned back in his seat, smiling. He wouldn't mind marrying Eli, but for now, this was perfect. He didn't need anything more. He didn't need a ring on his finger to know Eli loved him and that they were forever. He had everything he'd ever wanted and needed, and he was perfectly happy with his life the way it was.

YOU MAY ALSO ENJOY THE FOLLOWING FROM EXTASY BOOKS INC:

Lorcan
Catherine Lievens

Excerpt

Devon was an idiot. He needed to stay away from men, not to notice them. He wasn't in the market for a relationship, and he doubted he ever would.

Why couldn't he help but notice Lorcan, then?

Justin wouldn't be friends with someone as bad as Elroy. Hell, Justin wouldn't be friends with anyone who was an asshole. That meant Lorcan was probably safe, or as safe as any person could be. Still, that didn't mean Devon needed to think about him as a possible boyfriend.

He couldn't help it, though. Something inside him warmed when he was with Lorcan, and he couldn't explain it. He felt like he needed to talk to the man, to find out more about him. Did Lorcan have a boyfriend? A girlfriend? When had he become an enforcer? Did he find Devon attractive?

Devon's cheeks heated, and he focused on the food he was plating. He had to stop thinking about this. Even if he were in the mood for a relationship—which he definitely wasn't—why would Lorcan want him? He was an idiot. He'd stayed with an abusive man even though he'd been hurt. Who would want to be with him when he couldn't even take care of himself, let alone someone else? Certainly not Lorcan.

Lorcan was an enforcer, which meant he was smart. He deserved to be with someone just as smart as him. Hell, he could probably have anyone he wanted. He was a gorgeous man, with dark curls and dark eyes. He made Devon want to curl against him, and it took everything Devon had to stay away from him.

It was hard, though. Lorcan wasn't only gorgeous. He was also quite adorable, especially in the way he treated Devon. Devon had caught him staring a few times, and every single time, Lorcan looked away and blushed. It was like he wanted to talk to Devon, to be close to him, but Devon had a hard time believing that.

Lorcan probably had questions about Devon's past. He might want to know if Devon had heard about Elroy again, if he knew anything more than he had when he'd talked to Alpha Rhett. Devon had to convince himself of that before he did something stupid.

He didn't understand why he felt the way he did. He didn't have an explanation for it. He tried to ignore it during dinner, but it was hard. It was so hard that Yedley noticed something, and once they were in the kitchen alone again after dinner, he moved closer. "Is everything okay?" he asked.

Devon nodded. "Of course."

"You've been quiet." Yedley softly snorted. "I mean, you've been quieter than usual."

"I'm sorry," Devon murmured.

Yedley shook his head and squeezed Devon's arm. "It's not a bad thing. I don't expect you to have long conversations with me. I'm starting to get to know you, and I know it's not your thing. But I'm worried. Shouldn't we have asked our friends to come over for dinner? Is that what makes you uncomfortable?"

Devon shook his head, then nodded. It made Yedley laugh,

and Devon couldn't help but smile. "Okay, so maybe their presence makes me nervous. It doesn't mean you have to kick them out, though."

"I wouldn't say we're planning on kicking him out. But I'm sure that if we explained the problem, they'd understand."

"I don't want you to have to give this up because I'm around. They're your friends. You're allowed to ask them over for dinner, and they're allowed to be here and to enjoy it."

"But you're my friend, too. If what you need is to be left alone, we'll ask the others to leave."

Devon shook his head. "I know they won't hurt me. You wouldn't be friends with them if they did." He hesitated. Yedley probably didn't have an answer for him, but maybe he would have an idea of why Devon felt the way he did when it came to Lorcan. Devon was only human. Yedley might not be a shifter, but he was a Nix. "I just feel weird when Lorcan is around," he admitted.

Yedley cocked his head. "Can you elaborate? Weird can mean a lot of things."

"I'm not sure myself. I feel I should talk to him. My stomach flutters and I want to be close to him. I know it doesn't make sense since I don't know him. Do you think there's something there? I mean, why do you think I feel this way?"

Yedley bit his lower lip. Devon could tell from his expression that he probably wouldn't like what he was about to say, but he needed to know, so he waited, holding his breath.

"Have you thought about the fact that Lorcan might be your mate?" Yedley eventually asked.

Devon snorted so loudly he was pretty sure Justin heard him from the living room. "That's not possible," he said.

Yedley cocked a brow. "It's not?"

"Of course not. Humans only have one mate, right?"

"Well, I think it's more complicated than that. Some of the people who live with the pack have a second mate."

Devon had never heard of that, and he had a lot of

questions. "Is their first mate still around, though?"

"No. Gentry's mate died some time ago." Yedley blinked. "Are you telling me you have a mate?"

"I do, and he's still alive."

"Do you want to talk about it?"

Devon never wanted to talk about Elroy, but Yedley deserved an explanation. "It's one of the reasons I stayed with Elroy as long as I did. We were mates."

Yedley looked at Devon for so long that Devon started to wonder what was going on, then, he asked, "Are you sure you were mates?"

Devon shrugged. "I can't exactly tell, can I? I'm human. But he told me we were mates, and since he's a shifter, it has to be the truth."

"Some shifters lie, you know. Maybe he was lying to you because he wanted to keep you around."

Devon's heart felt like it stopped in his chest. He'd been clinging to the knowledge of being Elroy's mate for so long. He couldn't believe he was considering the fact it might have been a lie. "You think he lied to me," he said.

"I think it would have been convenient for him to lie, yes. He wanted to keep you around, and the fact that supposedly you're his mate made that happen. You might have left sooner if you hadn't believed it."

Devon couldn't deny that. He'd been thinking the same thing a few minutes ago. "Still. How am I supposed to know if he was lying?"

"You just told me you felt drawn to Lorcan."

"I do."

Yedley nodded. "Feeling drawn to someone is a sign they might be your mate. It's harder with humans since they don't feel the bond as strongly as shifters do, but it might be an explanation."

Devon's world was flipped once again. He didn't know if it was a good or a bad thing, though. It could start a new part of Devon's life if he allowed it.

Everything was too complicated, though. He couldn't think about this right now, yet he also couldn't stop thinking about it. "What should I do?" He asked, his voice barely a louder than a whisper.

"Talk to him. He's the only one who can confirm whether or not you're mates. I know you don't trust him or anyone, really, but I promise you, Lorcan is a good person. He won't force you into anything. None of our friends will."

Devon knew he was right. He trusted Justin and Yedley, and if they trusted their friends, then so should Devon. It didn't make it easier. He couldn't imagine himself having this kind of conversation with Lorcan or with anyone. Still, if Elroy had lied to him, he wanted to know. He needed to know.

About the Author

Catherine is the creator of several series, most of them paranormal, including the Whitedell Pride Series and the Gillham Pack Series. While she graduated in translation, she decided to go the writer's way because it was more fun to create her own stories and characters.

She's been living in Italy for more than twenty years, but she's a daughter of the North—Belgium to be precise—and she misses it so much that she's already planning to move back.

She loves pizza—probably too much—her son, her pets, and of course, books. She sneaks some reading time into her schedule every time she has five minutes free from writing, demands from her various pets and son, and lastly, housework.

Connect with her:

lievens.catherine@gmail.com

BookBub: https://www.bookbub.com/authors/catherine-lievens

Website: https://authorcatherinelievens.wordpress.com/

Facebook: https://www.facebook.com/catherine.lievens.9

Facebook Group: https://www.facebook.com/groups/411788002341528/

Twitter: https://twitter.com/authorCLievens

Newsletter: http://eepurl.com/c-uvKn